DEVIL IN BRISBANE

THE DEVIL IN BRISBANE

EDITED BY ZORAN ZIVKOVIC

PRIME BOOKS AUSTRALIA

Prime Books
www.prime-books.com

CONTENTS

continued

To the wonderful people who devotedly organize the Brisbane Writers Festival.

INTRODUCTION

Anthologies—as it was scientifically established a long time ago—can originate in many ways. One of them, no less legitimate or appropriate than others, is by chance. And indeed, chance is mostly responsible for the anthology *The Devil in Brisbane*, which you are about to read.

In March 2004 I was invited to the Brisbane Writers' Festival. I accepted the invitation without hesitation, although at first I didn't know very much about the Festival itself. Usually I am not a precipitous man (that would be rather unseemly at my age) but how could I have resisted the temptation of visiting Australia—for all practical purposes another planet? Considering the general circumstances, it might have been my once in a lifetime opportunity to do that.

Besides, what could possibly have gone wrong? Although no longer very fond of traveling, particularly long journeys (also a feature of advanced age), I would, hopefully, somehow manage to survive the thirty-six-hour flight, and once in Brisbane, I would be among my tribesmen, fellow writers.

This idyllic illusion soon began to evaporate when I learned the details of my participation. I was supposed to take part in three panels and to conduct a masterclass. At first sight, nothing to worry about for an experienced lecturer with dozens, if not hundreds of similar appearances behind him. Yes, but all of them in my native Serbian! Only then did I realize the simple fact that at the Festival I would have to make my first ever public address in English.

I panicked and was briefly on the verge of informing the organizers that, alas, due to reasons beyond my control, I wouldn't be able to come to Brisbane. But then pride took the upper hand. Such a cowardly retreat wasn't typical of my character (not to mention my age). But even more importantly, Mia, my wife, without whom my trip to Australia was simply unimaginable, would never forgive me for backing out on such unacceptable grounds. (To be quite precise, *any* grounds would have been equally unacceptable to Mia . . .)

After considering the situation more calmly, I managed to find some extenuating circumstances. Firstly, nobody could expect me, a foreign guest, to be faultlessly fluent in English. What's more, my funny accent and even funnier errors, which were unavoidable, might just sound charming, at least to some extent and to benevolent ears. Lastly, since there were several panelists at each session, I wouldn't have to speak for very long.

The only remaining true problem was the masterclass. I was supposed to spend as much as seven hours with the attendants and to speak most of the time. Indeed, who else if not I? But that was only one part of the trouble. The other was that I had no experience whatsoever with masterclasses. The institution of creative writing workshops doesn't exist in my part of the world and I had only a vague idea of what it was all about.

Besides, I didn't know anything about the eleven attendants except that they had paid quite an amount for the masterclass and that they were, presumably, aspiring writers. I didn't have any idea about their expectations. It was quite possible that they would end up disappointed by what they got in return for their money. I tried to get some more information from the organizers, but they told me only that the attendants were "most probably" only beginners.

In the dense fog I was surrounded by, I devised a cunning plan. I decided to begin the session by reading my story "The Telephone." (Actually, by having it read by a native English speaker, for obvious reasons . . .) It wasn't a random choice. "The Telephone" is about a strange conversation an author suffering from writer's block has with the Devil himself. I assumed that the attendants must also be suffering from one of the many forms of writer's block, since if that weren't the case, they probably wouldn't need the assistance of a masterclass at all . . .

After the reading of "The Telephone" was over, the attendants were asked to write a variation of the same theme. And then the miracle began . . .

By coincidence (synchronicity?), the same morning I started to write this introduction, I got a private email from one of my master-class attendants. (I am very glad I am still in touch with most of them.) I hope she won't mind me quoting her words anonymously here because they so eloquently summarize the unique experience we all went through.

"I wonder sometimes about what happened that day. What are the chances of a group of eleven or so neophyte writers coming up with a number of almost publishable stories in an hour? I am wondering what you did to us, and if you had a direct line to the devil, or another angel. Or if it was your unconscious speaking to ours. It would be interesting to talk to other writers who have run workshops and find out if they have experienced a similar phenomenon—a sort of collective creative energy generated by having a huge amount of effort contained in a small room. However, my bet is that you somehow influenced the process."

I didn't influence the process, of course. Well, at least not in any rational, conscious way. But, as some of us happen to know, the ways of creative energy, individual or collective, are well hidden and far from rational. So, just maybe, the idea of my "unconscious speaking" to the attendants isn't only metaphorical. In any case, the results were beyond all my expectations.

Although not knowing beforehand what they would have to write, the attendants began to do it very diligently and after one hour we ended up with eleven completed stories. Then we left the classroom, found a very nice place in the shade of a huge tree on the lawn, sat down on the grass, and the aspiring writers started to read their stories. It didn't take me long to realize that these weren't beginners' works at all. On the contrary, in fact. The majority of stories were not only "almost publishable," but very much so.

Everything could have ended there, with my humble self having been impressed by what the attendants had produced. Indeed, one could hardly expect more from a masterclass. But this wasn't just an ordinary masterclass and I hadn't traveled half the globe just to be impressed and to leave. That wouldn't have been fair and just. I had to try to make the most of what chance had suddenly offered.

As soon as we heard the last story, I brought forward an idea that was unanimously accepted, although with some (reasonable) disbelief. How about collecting the stories in an anthology tentatively entitled *The Devil in Brisbane?* Being the foreign department head at Prime Books, I would strongly recommend to Sean Wallace, the man in charge at Prime, that he bring it out.

Of course, one can't make a serious anthology of only eleven brief stories. We needed more contributions and they were soon to come. While still on the lawn along the Brisbane river, my three guests and assistants at the masterclass, K. J. Bishop, Vanda Ivanovic and Grace Dugan—probably under the spell of what they had just witnessed—promptly agreed to provide their own stories on the same subject: a writer encounters the Devil in Brisbane.

That also wouldn't have been enough, but then Geoffrey Maloney—who had been greatly attentive and helpful during our stay in his beautiful city—came up with an excellent suggestion. How about soliciting contributions from members of the Brisbane speculative fiction community? That seemed only fitting in at least two ways.

Firstly, for all I knew most of them were very talented writers. Secondly, they all lived in the Brisbane area.

The latter became relevant since I realized that one of the unifying factors of the anthology should be the fact that the authors were familiar with the city, in the sense that they lived there or had at least visited it. Indeed, writing about the Devil in Brisbane without knowing the city itself wouldn't be very appropriate. In the same vein, I played briefly with the idea of asking the contributors to provide some evidence, however circumstantial, of their personal encounter(s) with the Devil, but eventually abandoned it, since that would be interfering too much with their privacy . . .

What soon followed my return from Australia was a digital avalanche of stories. It seems the Devil vs. writer theme fell on very fertile ground among the members of the Brisbane speculative fiction community. I was very pleased to include in the anthology almost all the submitted contributions, since, in my humble view, they fully deserved it. I ended up with a total of 30 stories, varying the pivotal motif, one which has challenged centuries of writers, from a multitude of original narrative angles.

Initially, I planned to order the stories so that first came those of the masterclass attendees, but then decided that the most democratic order would be alphabetical (regardless of what the Devil might think of democracy). That order proved to be convenient in another sense too.

Somehow, it seemed justified also to include "The Telephone," since, in a way, it started it all. But I didn't feel very comfortable about it because I've never really appreciated anthologists who are too vain to be able to avoid including their own stories. And then, quite suddenly, Mia came to my rescue, providing me with an elegant way out.

Out of the blue, she offered to write a story too. I must confess I didn't take her seriously, since she had never written any prose at all (Mia is a translator). In just a few days, however, her contribution was on my desk. Like any devoted husband I would have had no alternative but to join the long and glorious tradition of men who have betrayed all their ethical ideals for the love of their respective wives, but fortunately I didn't have to face that dilemma here. Mia's story happened to be good and I would have included it even if we had not been so closely allied.

It has an additional value: as you will see, it is quite fitting as the concluding story in the anthology. It was a very lucky coincidence that the alphabetical order also placed it there. However good Mia's story might have been, it would have been impossible for me to avoid accusations of nepotism, if our family name had begun with an "A . . . "

Although you see on the cover "Edited by Zoran Zivkovic," this anthology shouldn't by any means be credited only to my humble self. It would have been impossible without the precious contributions of my two assistant editors, Geoffrey Maloney and K. J. Bishop. Among other things, Geoff masterfully edited all the stories, while K. J. produced the excellent cover art. Additionally, both of them contributed stories to the project.

This doesn't mean, however, that they share any responsibility for *The Devil in Brisbane* anthology. Any criticism should fall only on my shoulders. On the other hand, if there happens to be some glory, we will—needless to say—share it equally among us.

Zoran Zivkovic
Belgrade, January 2005

A DEVIL OF A JOB

Thomas J. Banks

It is dawn on a Sunday morning. Outside the sun is breaking over the horizon, and the study feels deathly cold. I pick up my pen from where it rests on the wooden desk, open a drawer and pull out a pad of old creased paper. I finger the pen idly for a few moments before beginning to write. Once I start, I cannot stop. The scratching of the nib on the paper is the only sound that breaks the dusty silence of the room. The words pour from my pen. I write about my dreams, my semi-conscious thoughts. Several pages of manic scrawl later, I pause, uneasy.

"Good," a voice says, "now we are making progress."

I rub my eyes and squint into the bright rays of sunshine penetrating the darkness of the old study, the oak-lined walls absorbing the warm golden rays. "Excuse me?" I reply nervously. "Progress with what?"

"Progress with your ideas. And most of all, progress with your lack of conviction as to which way to split yourself."

"I don't understand," I reply sheepishly. "I fully understand where my commitments lie and, no, I don't feel split. It's *you* that keeps hounding me with this writing nonsense."

"Is that right?" the kind but firm voice says, then laughs. "But who am I?"

The muse, I think, looking around the room, but I was sure the voice wasn't inside my head; I heard the sound of the words hitting my eardrums. I try to picture what the person behind the voice might look like in the way one would imagine a radio presenter when having no clue to their physical appearance. Although I can't see anyone, I feel piercing eyes boring into me, trying to find what I so desperately wish to hide. I'm afraid if those eyes look too deeply they will see my indecision, my fears—even my neuroses that I feel are so obviously on display within my subconscious self.

I angrily strike out a hundred or so words.

"Better," comes the voice again. "At least some more movement on the page, and probably the best so far."

I feel annoyed, and defensive too. I've never offered this glimpse of my life to anyone. I begin thinking about houses and jobs that demand commitment, and finances that require attention. Students' papers lie on my desk unmarked, bills sit there unpaid. And, here I am, contemplating where my creative spark is going to come from for my next inane warbling. To top it all off, I'm being criticised by someone who I'm not even sure is real!

"So," comes the omnipotent voice again, "is negative energy how you react to anyone who criticises your work? Is it really that terrible that someone should try to help you in this self-indulgent and futile pursuit?"

"I don't need any help," I bark back. "I didn't ask for help . . . and anyway, what exactly do you mean 'futile'?"

"Ah ha, so there is doubt? If you don't want help or recognition, then why, pray tell, do you sit for hours scrawling in that dog-eared little notebook? What purpose does it serve? To what ends do you justify squandering away hours aimlessly scribbling? And to get annoyed with the term "futile"?"

I lead two lives. The one in this room today is the secret me. I enjoy it in a way, locking myself behind the heavy wooden door and hiding from reality. And I don't have to justify myself to anyone in my seclusion. "I enjoy it," I blurt out without thinking. "Nothing more than that."

"And you're content with that, are you? Content to take it to the grave with you?"

"I . . . I . . . I'm not really sure I understand," I stammer, becoming nervous.

"Life is lived once," instructs the voice resolutely. "Once and once only. And remember that 'once' is a word with no time limits attached—it can easily be twenty-seven years, if need be."

"Why do you say that?" I ask, a cold sweat breaking out over my body.

"Many people in this world do not live to see twenty-seven years. You are lucky and, yet, every day you choose to ignore this and concern yourself with petty, insignificant details. In the grand scheme of things none of it matters. In fact, in the grand scheme of things, *you* don't matter. But life matters, and squandering it is a crime."

"Well, what is squandering it?" I retort, feeling slightly affronted. "My job is okay, and I have a decent life . . . and I enjoy my spare time, locked away in my study."

"But are you contented? Are you satisfied with the fact that your writings may never be seen by eyes other than your own? Are you happy that your job is what defines you?"

"Yes . . . err . . . I mean no . . . umm . . . I mean I don't really know."

"Opportunities are few and far between and should not be wasted. Grasp every single one. And remember, everywhere you go and everything you do, I can see you . . . "

"And why should I do anything about it? Why should that bother me?" I shouted.

"It shouldn't," I reply to myself, staring hard into the mirror at a familiar reflection. "But it obviously does . . . "

Had I really been talking to myself this whole time? I looked around the room to see no sign of anyone else. Was the indecision in my life finally getting too much for me?

I remembered an old quote about being more disappointed by the things that you didn't do than the things that you did. I pondered this for a while and decided that perhaps it was time to heed this advice myself. I turned my pen to a new sheet of paper, and confidently began to write, "Re: Resignation from position of . . . "

GUNSLINGER

Lee Battersby

The guy was old, but sharp looking, really sharp. Fans normally smell of desperation and desire. He smelled of money. That alone was enough to mark him out as different. He slipped into the booth as if he had every right to disturb Jake's breakfast, and coughed a short, sharp, attention-getting cough.

Jake lay down his copy of *Writer's Digest* and appraised the intruder. Grey hair swept back in a stylish cut, close cropped moustache making the transition to silver, handsome face that bore deepening lines around the eyes and mouth with casual grace. He wasn't carrying any extra weight either, the way a lot of middle-aged fans do. He appeared slim, almost muscular, although in a suit that expensive, it would be hard to tell either way. Fabric so black would have to cost serious bucks.

"Jake Tarrant." The voice was deep and burred, like gravel-rash on raw flesh. Jake suppressed a shiver. There was something singular about this approach. No "Hey, you're Jake Tarrant!" or "Excuse me, Mister Tarrant, may I have your autograph?" Just his name, spoken like a discovery.

"Can I help you?"

"I'm a fan of your work."

"Um, thank you." Jake made vague gestures towards the cooling remnants of his full English breakfast. "Can I . . . ?"

If his visitor noticed, he gave no indication. "High Noon, two guys at either end of the main street, 'Draw!' All that stuff. Tell me, do you really think it happened that way?"

Jake shrugged. "I . . . well, you have to take a little artistic license. There are conventions . . . "

"Conventions? Ha. I don't know much about conventions. But I *do* like Westerns."

The old guy glanced down at his right hand; fingers spread wide on the tabletop. Jake followed his gaze. The nails were long, perfectly manicured, sharp as rapiers. A signet ring crouched over the little finger. The design caught Jake's attention, and his breath caught in his throat.

"What the . . . ?"

"Gunslingers are the best characters, don't you think?" The voice was warm with good humour, but it was heat born of lava and sulphur. It washed over Jake like a physical thing, rising from the ring. "The loner comes into town, challenges the local hero, never knowing whether he's fast enough or whether he's slipped that fatal inch, become just one second too slow. That's life, I believe. Right on the edge of losing everything. That's when you're really alive."

Jake tore his gaze away from the terrible ring, only to be captured by the old guy's eyes. They bore the age of pyramids, or dinosaurs, or something immeasurably deep, and ancient, and inhuman. The irises were black, as deep as the black of his suit. Two red dots floated at their centres.

"Who . . . who are you?"

"You know."

Jake laughed, a hollow little sound. "Come on. Every Con I go to there's some guy wandering around dressed up like 'Scary Costume

Guy'. You can buy contact lenses, that's it, contact lenses, and that ring . . . "

Jake slid sideways, eyes searching for a security guard. This was a writers' festival, for God's sake. There should be protection against stalkers, here of all places. The stranger reached out and gently touched Jake's shoulder. A bolt of something electric snapped through his nervous system, leaving behind undeniable knowledge. He stiffened.

"Sit down, Jake."

Jake fell back into the seat, eyes wide. When he could trust himself to speak without screaming, it came out as a whisper.

"What do you want with me? I . . . "

"I'm told that for a writer to really understand his work he has to get inside the head of his characters, live a little of their lives. Is that true?"

Jake tried to nod, to move his head away from the frightful gaze, but his body would not respond.

"I'm told you even learnt to shoot."

"I . . . it was trap shooting. Just pistols. A bit of paintballing. I'm not . . . "

"I think you've got something I haven't had in a very long time, Jake. I've been looking for a challenge. And I think you're it." The old guy stood. "Brace yourself, pardner. I'm calling you out."

The heat was infernal. Sweat pricked Jake's skin and immediately soaked through his shirt. He raised a hand to wipe his forehead. It bumped against a hat brim. Jake frowned, and took it off. It was a Stetson, white leather gleaming in the sunlight. Jake looked at it in shock, then down at his clothing. His shirt and jeans had been replaced by a complete cowboy outfit. Everything was white; waistcoat, chaps, boots. A gun belt circled his waist, hung low and loose. A revolver lay inside a holster at his right hip. A silver star sat on his chest, the word 'Jake' etched into its centre.

"Like it?"

The Devil stood a few feet away. He too was dressed like a cowboy. His garb, however, was jet black. Two pearl handled revolvers hung in holsters, ready to be drawn in a cross-hand grip. Instead of a sheriff's star, he bore a badge in the shape of an inverted cross. Jake walked stiffly across to him.

"What's going on here?"

"I told you. I like Westerns. And I want a challenge. Now . . . " He looked around at the empty plain. "We need an appropriate venue, don't you think?"

He snapped his fingers. A dirt street spread itself out beneath them, radiating outwards from the old man's boots like a stain. Wooden buildings rose to either side. Signs hung from eaves, proclaiming the saloon, the leather goods store, the undertaker. Horses whinnied where they stood at railing posts. At the far end of the street, the church appeared, its cross a mirror of that on the old man's chest. By the time he realized what was happening, Jake was surrounded by a town straight out of Hollywood's idea of the Old West. Only one thing spoiled the illusion: every surface in the street was painted a bright whorehouse red.

"What . . . ?"

"Stole it from 'High Plains Drifter'." The Devil smiled his feral smile. "Still, you've got to admit it's appropriate. Remember what old Clint renamed the place? Besides, I think it looks homey."

Jake stood silent. The Devil saw the look of confusion on his face and sighed.

"Okay. Come with me, and I'll tell you why."

He strode toward the saloon and pushed through the bright red doors. Jake watched him go then followed, head down. His adversary was waiting inside, standing proudly behind the bar. A bottle of whisky and two glasses stood before him. He motioned Jake to a stool and poured two shots.

"All right then." He leaned on the bar. "Pour out your troubles, pardner. That's what we bartenders do, isn't it, listen to troubles?"

Jake swallowed his whisky in a single gulp and slammed his glass down.

"Why are you doing this to me?"

The Devil drained his glass and poured them both a refill.

"Do you know how many people I've killed? How many soldiers I've beaten at chess? How many kids I've out-hopscotched, how many golden fiddles I've offered and kept through the ages? I do. I remember every single one of them. In perfect detail." He drank, and poured another. "That's one of the things the storybooks don't mention, the perfect memory. It should be obvious. Anyway, I remember it all. Every bargain I've brokered, every deal I've cut, every favour I've granted. And they've all ended the same way. Every single one of them." He sighed, a melodramatic exhalation. "Nothing is interesting once you realize the outcome can never change."

"But . . . Why do you do it?" Jake was interested, despite his fear.

"Why?" The response was one of genuine surprise. "You know, nobody's asked me that before." He looked into his glass for a few seconds. "I'm not entirely sure what you think I am, Jake. I mean I *am*, but I'm also not. You'll understand that soon, one way or another."

"What do you mean?"

"Ever watch Doctor Who?"

"Yeah. When I was a kid."

"Who was your favourite?"

"Jon Pertwee. Easy. Why?"

"What about Bond movies?"

"Connery, of course."

"Tarzan?"

"I don't know. Um, Christopher Lambert?"

"Really?"

"I don't know." Jake shrugged in frustration. "What's it go to do with anything?"

The Devil snorted, and wiped at an imaginary stain on the countertop.

"I haven't always done this, you know. Yes, I know what you *think*." He raised a hand to stop Jake's protest. "But that's only some of it. Part of me has always been what you think I am, but there is another element." He looked down at his white hands. "Pertwee, Troughton, McGann, they were all different people and all the same. And when they got tired of being the Doctor they moved on. Connery, Moore, Dalton, they all got to stop being Bond. Part of me gets tired too. Part of me wants to stop."

"What do you mean?"

"Oh, you know." His eyes lost focus. "Tired of the bargaining. Tired of the hatred. Tired of wishing you could remember who you were before you became the latest chapter of someone else's story." He turned his ancient gaze back to his young customer. "Tired of wandering from soul to soul and never knowing when your concentration will slip, when you'll be that half second too slow, and it'll be you instead of them. Tired of being . . . "

"A gunslinger?"

The Devil smiled, a warm, friendly smile. "Yes. A gunslinger. Speaking of which." He walked out from behind the bar. Standing in the middle of the empty saloon, he tilted his head back, and called out in a strange and ugly voice.

"Hola! Hola! Hola, you demons and you devils. Come out and bear witness. The game is to be played again. Hola and attend!"

They came to him. From darkened corners and corners grown dark, from rooms along the balcony above his head and from between the floorboards beneath his feet, the inhabitants of his realm came to the Devil's call. Jake's skin froze at the sight of their malformed, night-marish features. His hand reached for the whisky bottle of its own accord and raised it to his lips. A long draught of searing liquid did little to suppress his urge to scream.

"Now, my little ones," the Devil said, stroking gently the heads of those nearest him, "the challenge awaits. Outside, in the street. Bear witness, so it is a true and just contest. And my darlings, I expect dress standards to be maintained."

Jake blinked, and in that time he and his adversary were again alone. Lucifer turned burning eyes and a sharp smile upon him.

"Well, the time for niceties is over, I'm afraid. Let's see the end of this." He raised his hand.

"Wait!"

"Yes?"

"I never . . . " Jake swallowed and tried again. "I never agreed to this. I thought a challenge had to be accepted. I never said I'd do this."

"Really? You thought that? After all those confrontations you've written, all those poor farmers forced to pick up guns when all they want to do is walk away back to their farms and the loving embrace of their good little wives?" The Devil took a last shot of whisky, then threw the glass in a perfect loop to smash in the fireplace at the far end of the saloon. "I thought you'd know better."

Jake stood at the end of the main street and gazed at the town spread out before him. To either side crowded his adversary's pets, leaning out of windows, standing on footpaths, peeking through doorways. He ran his eyes along their ranks. Each monstrosity had dressed in period clothing, as if it were normal for demons and nightmares to belong to such a town. Cowboys, preachers, native scouts abounded. Several schoolchildren were being herded toward a safe spot by a schoolmarm with a mass of writhing tendrils where her head should be.

The white-clad gunfighter walked slowly up the street, his audience growing silent as he passed, their grotesque heads turning to follow his progress. He stopped outside the saloon. Twenty yards away, another gunman stood, dressed entirely in black. The sun glinted from the inverted cross on his chest.

"Ready?"

"No."

"Too late."

The black figure moved to the centre of the dusty street, stood with hands held away from his sides, fingers splayed.

Jake saw them curling and uncurling in anticipation. The Devil's ancient eyes stared into Jake's young, frightened ones. The world fell away. The universe compressed upon itself until only the yards between Jake and the gunslinger remained. Darkness rose on either side of them, until the town existed alone inside a globe of pure empti-ness. All noise ceased. The Devil inhaled once, twice, then smiled.

"Draw!"

Jake's arm swung downwards. The palm of his hand slapped the side of the revolver. Fingers wrapped round the butt. The weight of the gun swung up and out of its holster. His left hand rolled over, heel striking the hammer and forcing it back. His trigger finger spasmed. *Pull, don't snatch. Pull, don't snatch*, a hidden part of his mind screamed. He felt the kick as the gun fired. The recoil blew his arm up and backwards. He heard, at a subconscious level, the bang-bang-bang of three shots being fired almost simultaneously.

The world fell still for a fraction of a heartbeat.

Then the first bullet hit him, and the second. For an eternity they bit into his flesh, ripped and tore through muscle and bone, blew exit holes in his back to make their escape. A scream began, and ended at the edge of the world. Jake fell, and the hard street thudded into him. His sight shrank until he could see only the black sky directly in front of his eyes. Coldness blew through him, and his breath echoed inside his skull.

A fuzzy, tear-blurred shape appeared. Jake blinked, and it resolved itself into his adversary. The Devil stood with one hand over the left side of his chest where the inverted cross had been. A small, pained grimace twisted his lips.

"Well, that was fun," he said. "You did it. You actually did it."

Jake tried to make his tongue work, tried to clear the blood from inside his mouth. After the fourth attempt, he coughed, and managed to drag out a single word.

"Wh . . . why?"

"Why you?" The Devil smiled a smile of love, and held his left hand away from his chest, palm outward, revealing the crimson blood in which it was coated. "Hope."

His eyes rolled upward into his head and he fell forward and out of Jake's vision.

Jake opened his eyes. For long seconds, he sat perfectly still, the memory of dying too fresh for him to recognize the sensation of living. When at last he was able, he reached up and explored his face with white, long-nailed hands. There could be no doubt. He was alive.

He turned his head and took in his surroundings. He was in the hotel, sitting inside a cubicle in the empty dining room. From outside, he could hear the sounds of traffic. It was still morning.

A body sat across from him. A thickset man, wearing a shirt and jeans. He lay slumped against the seat, eyes closed. A crimson stain wet the shirt on the left side of his chest. Jake frowned, recognition flickering at the edges of his memory. A voice inside him said, "Not entirely what you think I am. You'll find that out one way or another."

Jake caught a glimpse of himself in the mirror above the buffet: the grey hair in its stylish cut, the handsome face bearing a silvering moustache. A signet ring burned at his finger. Jake had never seen such a beautiful object. It offered him absolution, the acceptance of things he would soon come to understand.

He smiled. He knew one thing: this was the way it had been since the dawn of time. When one was finished, another took up the mantle. He drank from the glass of pineapple juice next to the dead man's breakfast. It was time to leave. A part of his soul was pulling him away from this place. Somewhere in Japan, a young boy was watching his father practice archery. He was wishing with all his heart that he could one day be as good. Jake nodded.

"Okay, then," he said, and the old guy in the mirror mouthed the words back at him. He stood and moved to the door, opened it and walked through. Without a backward glance, the Devil went into the night.

AN INNOCENT TÊTE-Â-TÊTE WITH THE DEVIL

Celeste Birt

The phone rang again; it was the third time today.

I answered.

"You called?" said the devil in a deep and dreary voice.

"Yes," I replied. I wasn't ashamed that I'd called on the devil. I mean, people call on God all the time. And, well, um, the devil once sat to the left of God. Right?

Secretly I didn't expect a reply—you never do.

"Well?" the devil asked.

"Well," was all I could say.

"Well?" he asked once again.

"I . . . I was wondering." Pause. There was a quiver in my voice and I was sounding more like a naughty schoolgirl than a serious interlocutor. I forced myself to speak again, this time quickly and without pause. "I would appreciate your assistance and cooperation with a plan that has to do with my future success and which may possibly alter the history of all mankind."

"You would appreciate *my* assistance," he repeated.

"Yes," I replied confidently.

"Do you intend to elaborate?" he asked.

"Yes, of course, sorry. As you may know I am also a very busy person. I am a writer, or at least I aspire to be. And yet I still don't quite understand how what I would like to be, but aren't quite yet, or indeed may never be, defines who I am. However, we all must be something or somebody. Don't you agree?"

He asked again without the slightest deviation in his voice, "You would appreciate *my* assistance?"

"Yes. I was just about to get to that." Or was I? Perhaps I am rambling to stall time. My conscience begins to rear its annoying head. "Is talking to the devil immoral?" it asks.

"Define moral!" I mentally shout back.

"Am I a good person?"

"Define good!" I retaliate.

"Would my mother approve?"

"Would God approve?"

Yes, the question is rhetorical, but I am desperate enough to defy my conscience, God, even my mother.

Here goes . . .

"I would greatly appreciate your assistance in eradicating all other writers from the face of the earth, all canon texts, all myth, in fact everything which has ever been written since the beginning of time and before that."

"Interesting," he said. "Why?"

"So that I may write without the burden of doing better or worse than those who have gone before me."

"This is impossible, even for me," he replied.

"Fine!" I shouted. "Hang up and don't ever return my calls again!"

"No, you hang up first," he said.

I threw the phone against the wall and slumped into my corduroy beanbag. I knew I was asking for too much, but the world asks too much of me. From birth, the expectations were clear: do something extraordinary, something great and meaningful, something which is beneficial to mankind. Why do we live our lives fearing, planning, and anticipating the future? Yet I can't stop wondering what I'll do, or be, or see, or achieve.

Perhaps I will write—with or without the devil's assistance.

The phone rang again.

BETWEEN THE COVERS

K. J. Bishop

The burgundy leather armchair supported me like a large, luxurious, paternal lap. A pair of Chinese lanterns cast meditative light on William Morris wallpaper, floral Axminster carpet, handsome walnut furniture and a slight overprofusion of objets d'art. Numerous bookcases lined the walls, as could be expected in the consulting room of one who was a friend to writers. The air was slightly on the warm and stuffy side. Against the wall, to my right, stood a small bookcase holding Sanskrit volumes, with a painting of striped tulips, by Bosschaert the Elder if I wasn't mistaken, hanging above. To my left, the lovely evening blues and purples of a Tiffany wisteria lamp competed ably with the tulips for the attention of my gaze. With such charming decorations to admire, you could forgive, and almost forget, the lack of windows in the room.

Facing me, in another armchair, sat my old friend the Devil. He was manifesting as civilised, affable Mephisto, in a grey silk suit, with small discreet horns and a narrow goatee.

I had armoured myself in my black, chic "The Author Wears Prada" costume.

"I'm so glad," the Devil said warmly, "that you've found something worthwhile to spend your royalties on. It must be wonderful to see your first novel doing so well."

"Doing well, thanks to you," I said.

The Prince of Darkness inclined his handsome head. "It was my pleasure."

I wasn't a Faust or a Paganini. The Devil had approached me, not the other way around. He had called me on the phone one night, telling me he'd secretly observed me writing the book, had read the finished manuscript when I wasn't around, and liked it so much that he wanted to promote it. He explained that he had a soft spot for writers in general. Quoting Mario Vargas Lhosa's description of the desire to write as a basic questioning of reality, the Devil called writing an act rooted in doubt. Doubt, of course, undercuts faith, and is therefore something that the Devil strives to foster in the world. He said that my book had an exceptional quota of doubt in it, which was true. Most of the characters were doubting types, the *mise en scène* was a dreamlike fantasy world, and there was considerable doubt as to the nature, and even the existence, of the plot. These factors had moved him to offer me his services.

He had rendered considerable assistance towards getting my book published (the present state of the publishing industry is such that an author, without a supernatural ally to intercede with literary agents, stands little chance of finding a publisher other than in the smallest of the small press). His famously persuasive tongue had whispered in the ears of reviewers and booksellers. As a result of the Devil's efforts, my novel had been a critical and commercial success.

"You know, I can't help wondering if I've sold my soul to you," I said. This wasn't what I'd really come to talk about, but it was something that had been niggling at me.

The Devil smirked sweetly. "Did we sign a contract?"

"No, but I don't have a written contract with my agent, either. He just sells my work and takes his fifteen per cent."

"Well, perhaps I own fifteen per cent of your soul," suggested the Devil.

I came to my main point. "Do you know what's been happening in my life these last two years?"

"Unlike some entities I could mention, I lay no claim to omniscience," replied the Devil. "So surprise me."

"First of all, I don't want you to think I'm complaining. I'm very happy with the way things have gone with the first book. But I've had an ongoing problem. An embarrassing problem, actually."

"*Liebling*, your embarrassment is my amusement. Entertain me."

"Well, I can't get it up."

The Devil gazed at my feminine form and archly arched a saturnine eyebrow.

"My pen," I clarified. "I haven't been able to get my pen up. Oh, sometimes I can make it work for a little while, long enough to do a short story or an article. But it hasn't been equal to the task of writing another novel."

"Ah. Aaaahhhh," the Devil said, drawing the syllable out like the bowels of St. Erasmus on the windlass. "Well, have you brought your pen with you? If you show it to me I might be able to tell you what's wrong with it."

I dug my pen out of my handbag and handed it to the Devil. He examined it from all angles. "It seems fine," he said. "I can't detect anything wrong with it. And I'm good at finding fault, you know."

"It isn't suffering from performance anxiety?" I queried. "After all, it wrote a successful book. Wouldn't it only be natural for it to feel nervous about the next one?"

"It doesn't feel a bit nervous to me," said the Devil. "And of course I'm good at inspiring nervousness, too. The fact that your pen is perfectly calm even with me holding it suggests that it possesses an unflappable disposition." He returned the pen to me and I placed it back in my bag.

"Then if the pen isn't the problem, it must be the books," I declared.

"The books? What books, and what sort of problem are they?" asked the Devil mildly.

Some writers are able to make their fictions out of what the world gives them—their lives, their daydreams, their observations of other people, their reading. Other writers must wait for unwritten fictions to come to them in the hope of being written. I am the latter sort of writer.

One night, when I was standing on the balcony of the small apartment my husband Ivan and I used to have, enjoying a smoke after a good dinner, a story appeared beside me. At that time I didn't think I was a writer at all. I had a job in an office, I painted and played netball on the weekends, and I certainly had never contemplated sitting down and writing a story either for pleasure or for profit. But one moment I was alone on the balcony and the next moment the unwritten story was there, right next to me, a few sheets of blank paper clipped together and supported on little spindly legs, telling me we'd both have some fun if I was willing to write it. Why not? I thought. As a student at school I had been good at English. I was quite an avid reader, particularly of fantasy and science fiction, and I felt I knew enough about literature to justify my trying out the writing side of it.

I took the story into the spare room. We sat on the bed, it dictated itself to me, and I wrote it down, following what it was saying as well as I could. As it happened, the story was a fantasy. It took me a few drafts before the story declared itself happy with my work. I typed the final draft into the computer (I always wrote longhand, only using the computer for this last stage), loaded the story's sheets of paper into the printer, clipped them together again when printing was done, and sent the story off to a magazine. The magazine accepted it, and six months later I was a published author.

After that, more stories came to me. I enjoyed the company of each one as I was writing it, but I never felt any pain when a story was completed and it and I had to part company. Our relationships were cordial but professional.

Then the novel came. I was leaning on the railing of the promenade beside the river after a typically unexciting day at work, enjoying the calm beauty of the evening. I heard a small noise to my right, looked that way, and saw a book standing there, balancing on little legs only marginally sturdier than those of its story-length kin. Its cover was blank, and as the breeze coming off the water ruffled its pages, I could see that they were blank too.

The unwritten book and I began talking. Well, flirting, really. The book was quite a charming Lothario. I found myself unable to object when it accompanied me to the railway station, nor when it climbed into the carriage with me. Nor could I bring myself to try to dissuade it from following me home. I wondered what Ivan was going to think. We were quite an ordinary couple. The stories had been brief flings, but a novel would need a much longer commitment. Was my husband ready for a *ménage à trois*?

As it happened, I got the book into the house without Ivan noticing. But as the book and I began to spend long hours in the spare bedroom by ourselves, he began to wonder what was going on, and one day he walked in on us. The book was sitting on the bed, dictating to me while I wrote in a notepad. (It is most unfortunate for books that they don't have arms, or they'd be able to write themselves.) I had fallen quite in love with the book, and wanted nothing more than to bring it into the world.

Happily, when I showed the draft to Ivan, he, too, fell in love with the book. For the next couple of years, he and I and the book were an amorous threesome. But once the book was finished, it left us. (Though I couldn't, of course, print directly onto the book itself, when I printed out the final manuscript the book gave a gallant little bow and vanished into thin air.)

Ivan took its departure philosophically, but I felt bereaved. Even though I was delighted to see its clones in bookshops, I missed the original book, and its daily revelations of itself, terribly.

When you've written one book the world at large expects you to keep writing books. I would have been happy to conform to this expectation, since I couldn't imagine any other occupation giving me as much pleasure as I'd enjoyed in the company of my paper paramour. A few stories came my way, but I'd lost the taste for brief liaisons. There was more duty than pleasure in writing them, and they seemed to notice. Perhaps word got around that I was no fun anymore, since the stories soon stopped coming. And, really, I wasn't much fun. I was getting depressed. I knew my state of mind would only worsen if I didn't find another book to fill the hole the first one had left.

I resorted to doing what many writers of my ilk must: I cruised for books. I soon came to recognise my own type. If you know what to look for, a writer in search of a book is easy to spot. We'll always be alone in a place where there aren't many other people, and you'll see us glancing often at the unoccupied spaces to either side of us. We don't crowd each other, the unspoken rule being that we don't remain stationary within each other's sight. To help books find appropriate writers, we have a hanky code. I wore a magenta hanky with pale blue checks, indicating my preference for speculative fiction and a secondary interest in general fiction.

I wasn't unlucky in the chase. Quite a few books approached me, and I took most of them home. The next part of the story was always the same. The book and I would retreat to the spare room. My pen would stir, and I'd write a few paragraphs. Most of the books were very pleasant company, and I felt that all their stories were worthy of telling. But I didn't fall in love with a single one of them. After those first few paragraphs, or, at most, a few pages, I would realise it. When books came along that resembled the first one closely enough to be sequels, as happened two or three times, it turned out to be like dating your ex-boyfriend's kid brother.

Most of the books left quietly when I told them I couldn't write them. A couple cried, making me feel terrible. One became violent and hit me over the head with itself.

By the time the first book had recouped its advance and I was earning royalties, I still hadn't found a second book to write. I was enjoying my new lifestyle, but my inner life was giving me no joy. I wondered if I should give up writing and try yoga instead. But I had long ago quit my office job, and I wasn't so rich that I could afford to retire. In any case, I didn't want to. Early mornings and late evenings found me lurking around suburban railway stations and lonely cafés, hanky displayed in the pocket of the old jeans I always wore on my amatory expeditions to make myself look like a struggling unpublished author. Successful writers are supposed to have books lining up outside their doors, begging us to write them, and I would have been embarrassed to reveal myself as one who had already struck it lucky in the literary world.

I still brought books home, but found myself decreasingly able do anything with them. A hundred words, fifty, ten—that was what my endurance dwindled to. This was when I began to wonder if there was something wrong with my pen. I didn't want to think that there had only been the one book that I was ever going to get excited about.

The Devil already knew about the first book (we'd briefly discussed the phenomenon of unwritten books in our phone conversation), and I gave him a précis of the rest.

"I even lost the energy to evict books that wanted to stay with me," I admitted in conclusion. " Four of them are still living under my roof. My husband treats them like pets, even though they're obviously taking advantage of his good nature. They've turned our flat into a pigsty. I can't bring other books home anymore. I have to take them to hotel rooms, and that costs money. I need to fall in love with a book again, and I don't think I can do it by myself. I need you to help me."

"I'm afraid," said the Devil, not looking afraid at all, "that what you're asking is the one thing I can't help you with."

"But why not?" I asked, flummoxed. Surely a love spell was within the Devil's capabilities.

The Devil grinned devilishly. "Because of our contract."

"But we don't have a contract. You said so."

"Actually, my dear, *you* said so."

I tried to remember, and had to concede that the Devil was right. I had been the one who said we didn't have a contract. But if we did have one, why couldn't I remember signing it?

"If we've got a contract, you must have a copy. Show it to me," I said.

"My pleasure." With a rather swishy flourish of his hand, the Devil plucked a piece of paper out of the air between us and held it out for me to read.

It was a very ordinary looking contract. No letters of fire, just Times New Roman. The signatures were not in blood but plain black ink. One was indisputably mine. The other was written in characters resembling fragments of circuit diagrams (or fancy pitchforks). Eyes better educated than mine could perhaps have read it. Or perhaps not.

There were only four paragraphs in the contract. The first contained the Devil's pledge to help me publish and promote the book to the full extent of his abilities. In the second paragraph, I granted him fifteen per cent of my soul. In the third paragraph, I granted something additional: I would never be able to fall in love with another unwritten work of fiction. The fourth paragraph stipulated that the Devil would cause me to forget that the contract existed, for a period of three years or until I contacted him with a request for aid in respect of my lack of romantic enthusiasm for unwritten literature.

Would I miss fifteen per cent of my soul? Surely not, I tried telling myself. I might even be able to claim it as a tax deduction. Trying to summon up a bit of inner bravado, I made a mental note to ask my accountant about the value of a soul. But as for the third paragraph, I couldn't believe I'd agreed to such a thing.

"I've forgotten why I wanted to forget," I said, "but I can guess that I wanted some time to enjoy my success without worrying about the future."

The Devil smiled and nodded and I contemplated the irony.

"You thought you'd be able to write without being in love," he said. "Most writers are able to. You expected to regain your professional attitude."

"What happened?" I asked. "Am I going to get my memory back now?"

"I can't restore the memory I extracted, but it will only take me a minute to explain," the Devil replied. "You did, in fact, make a contract with me, as you have seen. You summoned me with a quaint old spell. Presumably you didn't know that I'm listed in the Yellow Pages. You were so besotted with your book that you couldn't face the prospect of it not being successful in the world. It wasn't so much for your own sake as for the book's that you wanted my help. Rather touching, really. The part where you only fall in love with a book once in your lifetime is a modification of the first contract I offered you, in which I asked for forty per cent of your soul. You declined the only other option I was able to offer."

"Which was?"

"The end of your marriage. You'd have fallen for another book, and your husband would have grown jealous and filed for divorce."

At least I could say I felt no regret about turning that option down.

"Why only forty per cent of my soul?"

"I gave up demanding entire souls quite a long time ago. People always wanted too much in exchange. They demanded lifetimes of debauchery, bottomless bank accounts, journeys to other planets—you name the extravaganza, I've arranged it for someone. The crafty ones always want peace of mind into the bargain, too. It just wasn't worth it on my part, particularly as most of the people who entered into contracts with me were going to end up in Hell anyway. So

I started experimenting with flexible contracts, offering more modest services in exchange for a percentage of the soul—sometimes combined, as in your case, with other commodities of exchange. And it worked wonderfully. I found millions of people willing to give me a part of their soul in return for quite small services. Believe me, the parts add up."

"And what about the part that's left? Can it regenerate the lost portion, like a liver will?" I shook my head at my own question. "It can't, can it?"

"If you'd taken the peace of mind clause, you'd believe that your soul will regrow the part I take. But that clause costs an extra ten per cent, and you decided against it. You know the truth, and you'll have to live with it."

"And what about your phone call—just an act?"

"A little charade, but performed with a sincere spirit. I do have a soft spot for writers, and I did like your book, which is why I let you have such easy terms. You'll never love a book again, but in exchange for that you kept an extra twenty-five per cent of your one and only, precious soul."

"And your gain—the commodity of exchange—is that for the rest of my life I'll be yearning for another love affair with a book, and you'll get your jollies from watching me suffer."

The Devil licked his sensual lips. "There's another reason why I like writers. You're so very easy to torment. All I have to do is deny you things that most people never dream of having in the first place."

I ignored the jibe. " What about my copy of the contract?" I demanded. "Shouldn't I have one?" I couldn't remember seeing a copy in my files. But then, how often did I look through my files?

"Your agent has it, so that you wouldn't find it accidentally before your three years were up," the Devil answered with an air of slightly tried patience.

I could feel the calmness of shock wearing off and the unpleasant beginning of tears niggling at my throat and eyes. I wanted to leave before I cracked. I got up from the chair.

"Before you go," said the Devil, "permit me to give you some advice. Don't worry too much about your soul. Personal identity is merely fiction, after all, as any number of writers have deduced. This illusion you call identity is a grab-bag of fleeting sensations, imagination, and the reconstructions known as memory. Think how much of yourself you've already lost, or failed even to construct, through lack of will, creativity and recall."

With those comforting words ringing in my ears, I found myself standing in the basement car park of the anonymous office building in which the Devil's consulting room was located. I walked to my car, and sat in the driver's seat and had a good cry. I even banged my forehead against the steering wheel a few times, though quite gently, so as not to accidentally set off the airbag.

I drove home, hands trembling on the wheel and gearstick, feet trembling on the pedals. Luckily I didn't live too far away. Whilst in the car, I wondered where the percentage of my soul that remained mine was heading for. I thought gloomily about the Prada and the camel and the eye of the needle, and I realised that I was going to change my ways. I was too scared not to. And what about Ivan? If we were to be together in the afterlife, what would it be like for him if I was only eighty-five per cent there? Even if I wouldn't miss fifteen per cent of my soul, perhaps he would. I began to feel quite ill with worry and guilt.

I arrived home at around 3 p.m. Ivan was still at work. The four books that wouldn't go away were lying around in the living room, where they were camping. They no longer resembled the pristine blank-paged hardbacks I'd picked up. They were dishevelled, dirty, dog-eared. They smelled, and the room smelled of them; overflowing ashtrays and empty beer cans were scattered all around them. They didn't greet me. They'd stopped talking to me. They only communicated with Ivan, who made their beer runs.

But if I was going to keep writing, I had to write one of them. You still can do it, you know, I told myself. Now that you're aware of the situation, you can accept it. You don't need to be in love. Comradeship and a sense of duty can take the place of passion. In fact, they're often more useful than passion, in the long run. You just need some discipline. Application of the seat of the pants to the seat of the chair, and all that.

Pep talks usually disgusted me, and I expected to be disgusted by that little effort of mine. But instead, a slightly wonderful thing happened. I looked around at the four unwritten books and felt a surge of compassion. In part it was plain pity that I felt, but there was a sense of empathy as well. What was I, if not an unfinished project? Worse, an unfinishable project, since death is only a truncation, and only in the case of certain suicides a carefully worked conclusion, to the story of a life. I suddenly envisioned myself as an illusion with a comradely interest in other illusions.

I was moved to say to the books, "I'm sorry. I've been selfish and unreasonable."

The books remained silent in their postures of decrepit indolence. I wasn't discouraged. I'd found a straw I could clutch at, and I was going to clutch like mad in the hope that it was a good, strong, secure straw. Because I didn't love these books, it occurred to me that it would be a nobler thing and a more rigorous exercise of my skill to write one of them than to write a book that was easy to love.

I had crafted the first book with almost delirious pleasure, but what about crafting myself? If I was a being with a soul, surely that soul was as important as a book. If I was only an illusion, didn't I want to be a beautiful illusion? Had the first book perhaps been something of a demon lover, and was the real challenge not to keep looking for that lover again but to make myself into a creature of comparable charm? Because at the moment, the hard voice of reality said, I was a bit of a shit.

Everything that had happened today had steered me towards this thought. By the distinct whiff of piety in it, I felt justified in wondering—clutch that straw!—if the being with whom I had been dealing was really the Devil. What if there was a larger self-deception surrounding the one involving the contract? What if the entire thing was something I'd elaborately contrived to stretch myself as a writer and raise my standards of behaviour?

I decided to call my agent's office. His assistant answered the phone. I asked her if she could look through my file for a contract concerning my soul.

Yes, she said, it was there.

"Are you able to find out for me whether that's actually the Devil's signature?"

"Certainly," she replied.

"Really?"

"Of course. Writers are always making contracts with the Devil and then wishing they hadn't," she said breezily. "They hope the Devil's signature is fake, and ask us to find out."

"Has it ever been fake?"

"I don't think so, but there's always a first time. Shall I fax it to the person who handles verifications of this sort?"

I hesitated. If the signature was authentic, I'd be miserable. If it was a fake, or the signature of a benign power, I'd very probably relax and continue to search foolishly for another great romance between the covers of an unwritten book. Finally, there was the possibility that the signature might be part of the putative deception, a fake good enough to deceive an expert.

"I'll think about it," I said.

"Of course," said the assistant, sounding as if she had expected my response. We said goodbye and I hung up.

A writer needs a good imagination, and a writer of speculative fiction needs a particularly good one. Whatever my other shortcomings, my imagination was fairly well developed. And just as a sprinter's strong legs don't weaken between races, a strong imagination operates outside the hours when it's being used for creative work. Shaken up as I was, I knew that in time my imagination would convince me either that the Devil hadn't been the Devil, or that the whole thing had been a particularly vivid flight of fancy. The episode with the Devil now belonged to memory, and one can sometimes doubt whether a memory is of a real event or of a dreamed or imagined one, particularly if the event is strange. Moreover, a memory becomes slightly distorted each time it is examined, and I knew I would be examining the memory of my conversation with the Devil many, many times. A day would certainly come when I would seriously doubt its authenticity, and, after that, a day when I would dismiss it altogether. In time, therefore, I'd have my peace of mind.

But I didn't have it yet.

I set my eyes on the lousiest looking of the four books and began to navigate my way towards it through the reefs of ashtrays and cans. The book regarded me in a deeply cynical way, as it had every right to. But it was far smaller than I, and it was too drunk to resist me. Essaying a Byronic mien, I knelt before the book, swept it up in my arms, grabbed a beer for it from an open six-pack parked nearby, carried it into the spare room and shut the door. I didn't bother with the pen. I went straight to the computer keyboard.

A little under a year later, my second novel was published. Contra to the expectations of readers and critics, it was not a fantasy but a romance of sorts about an odd couple who break the bylaws of literature by not falling in love.

THE BLANK PAGE

Michele Cashmore

The first time I saw him, I was sitting in the park below the windmill observatory. I had just finished flicking through a magazine and was trying to write in my diary. It was perfect there, underneath the jacaranda, its umbrella of lilac blossom providing cool shade against the heat of a typical Brisbane afternoon. I had a bench seat all to myself, escaping reality and the peak lunch hour.

I will never forget him as he came from the direction of Albert Street. He was gorgeous; tall, and muscular, with olive skin. His black hair, tied in a plait, fell below his waist. His jeans hugged his hips. A thick leather belt straddled his pelvis. A black T-Shirt clung to his chest and spread tight across his firm abs. As he moved closer, he looked at me with such deep brown eyes. They smouldered beneath the shadow of his cap and I felt totally lost just looking into them. My eyes broke contact with his when he rolled his tongue across his teeth, licking his lower lip. When he smiled, his lips were full with desire but then, before I knew it, he walked away, toward Upper Edward Street, leaving me feeling exasperated.

And now a week later, I find myself here, waiting at the same bench, looking for him. I feel shaky, adrenalin is pumping through my veins at the mere possibility of seeing him again. It's quite bizarre really, because no-one has ever made me feel this way. I take deep breaths and finally my nerves begin to settle. Frustration is setting in thick and fast as I struggle to find words to put on paper. Other faces push past me: cyclists, a few joggers, mothers with prams—office workers jostle between park and street.

Every Wednesday, this is a ritual for me, a midweek break from my boring job as an accounts clerk. I sit and write in my diary, which essentially is my novel. I'm writing a novel about . . . well, no, I don't want to give it away . . . let's just say, I'm writing my novel. Yes, another novel. I find it easier to write in the park. I can take the smells and sights of the cityscape, and breathe them into my story. It's my third novel, but that doesn't really count, because I haven't been published yet. I know I will be; it's all just a matter of time. I shake my head with annoyance as my wrist eventually gives in to writer's cramp. Huh, I've barely written a thing! I can't think straight, nothing is happening on the page, and I can't find him. My mind screams coffee. I realise that I'm not going to be graced by his beauty today, so I give up, pack up my pencils, diary and magazine. I swing my daypack on my back and, with a sigh, trudge towards Queen Street Mall.

It is hot today, hotter than normal; the heat sears my eyes and my singlet clings to my back. Sweat is dripping between my breasts and my hair sticks to my scalp and face where it has escaped my ponytail. I finally reach the bottom of Edward Street and my throat is parched. I started off this morning feeling fresh, invigorated and keen to see him again. I wore my faded blue jeans that neatly hugged my slim hips, my favourite red singlet and a thick silver chain that now annoys me as it cuts into my neck. I zigzag my way through the busy crowd until I find refuge in an open-air café in the mall. I take the seat with a corner table that faces the street, so I have a view of the constant throng of people going about their business. A waiter, all of about seventeen, with spiked blond hair and an eyebrow stud, approaches me with a beaming smile, asks if I would like to know the specials of the day.

"Coffee, please. Latte," I say.

He looks at me with his blue eyes and says, "No worries, I'll be right back."

I should've been having coffee in Borders Bookshop, so I could feel more in the writing mood. But Borders is too far away in this humidity and I'm thirsty. My latte arrives and I ask, "Please, can I have some water?"

"No problem."

Ten minutes later, a wine bottle of water and a dirty glass filled with ice arrive at my table. Beggars can't be choosers. I guzzle glass after glass, then I see him. He is right opposite, walking towards me. He smiles, and raises his eyebrows, thick and dark beneath his cap. He removes his shades and says, "Hi, can I join you?"

I have trouble engaging my mouth, but eventually when I can operate it in normal gear, I say, "Sure."

He doesn't bother with the entrance, instead he steps over the iron railing and seats himself at my table. He flicks his plait back over his shoulder and that's when I notice a gold chain around his neck. I'm instantly curious.

The same waiter asks "Can I get you anything, sir?"

"Yeah, I'll have a Fourex."

"No problem and, Ma'am, can I get you anything else?"

I stammer and say, "Ah, some more water would be great thanks."

"So what are you up to on such a gorgeous day?" this mysterious stranger asks, his eyes penetrating mine, his tongue licking his lower lip.

"Um, I have the day off today," I say awkwardly and begin to fidget in my seat.

"Oh? What do you do?"

"I'm a writer."

"A writer. Wow! Who do you work for?"

"No, I mean, um, yes, I'm a writer, but really I work for an accounting firm."

"Oh, I see." His smile broadens. "But you're a writer really."

"Yes," I answer, as my cheeks reach a full flush. "Gosh, it's so hot today, isn't it?" I say as I reach for the glass. Half melted ice cubes clink as I press it to my cheeks to ease the burn. I know I have gone bright red and even the coolness of the glass won't take it away.

"So what's your name?" I ask hesitantly.

"Hmm, what's your name?" he asked.

I take another gulp of water. I wish the sweat would stop dripping between my breasts. I so want to use my shirt to soak it up or grab a tissue to wipe it away but, of course, I can't.

"I asked first."

"My name is Caleb."

"That's a nice name." I wince at how stupid and lame I sound, so I hurriedly add, "My name is Lisa, nice to meet you." I hold out my hand, aware that it is clammy, but I hold it out anyway.

He clasps it firmly, smiles and says, "Nice to meet you too."

He takes his time to let go of my hand, all the while looking into my eyes as though he is searching for something.

Breaking the silence and the handshake, I say, "So what do you do?"

"Oh, me? A bit of everything."

"What do you mean?"

"Well, mostly, I look for writers." His beer arrives. He smiles cheekily, brings the cold bottle to his lips and sucks greedily until at least a third of the alcohol is consumed.

"Yeah, right." I laugh. "What do you mean you look for writers?"

"I crave imagination and new ideas; it's what keeps me alive." He picks up my hand and says, "Come on, why don't we go somewhere?"

"Like where?" I ask.

"Oh, I don't know. Let's go for a walk in the Botanical Gardens or something."

"Actually, I'm pretty tired. I think I need to be getting home." My head is spinning. I'm hot and nauseous. I'm afraid. I don't know whether I'm afraid of him or myself. Will I succumb to his seduction? Possibly. I'm not sure how I feel; all I know is that I have no idea who he is. And for a split second, I actually considered walking through the gardens with a complete stranger!

He tips his cap, takes another swig of his beer, licks his lips and says, "This one's on me." He places a twenty dollar bill beneath the empty glass.

He leans over and kisses me hard on the mouth, then says, "Perhaps we shall meet again." He gets up, smiles, steps over the railing and walks away. I watch, gob- smacked, as his lean body swaggers toward Queen Street. I want to jump up and follow him, but I don't dare. I don't even know who he is. I sit in silence for what seems a long time. The waiter takes the money and returns with change. I leave it on the table.

Heading back towards the windmill, I find myself another park bench. My usual spot is taken by two old women feeding pigeons, both plucking pieces of bread from uncut loaves and smiling as they throw them into the throng. In a daze, I rummage around in my bag, until I find my diary and pencil, but I can't think straight, I can't write. The blank page of my diary just stares at me, like this white piece of snow that never melts. The memory of his kiss lingers on my mouth. When my fingers touch my lips, they burn. Delicious tingles race up and down my spine. Caleb. The name resonates through my being and the heat from my body is not just from the day. I have to get home. Perhaps by then, my mind will clear enough for me to grasp what is happening. For now, my mind is blank. Who the hell is he? And what did he mean, he looks for writers? Oh, god! What if he was an editor or something and I had just let him go, because I was too damn infatuated with his good looks?

Berating myself, I head toward Central Station. I search the monitors for the next train to Cleveland and head for Platform 6. I enter the end of the carriage that has the least people, and find a double seat for the long journey home. Annoyed that I can't find a way to express how Caleb made me feel, I pull out my magazine instead. Flipping through the pages, my mind in a fog, I suddenly feel warmth against the back of my neck. I turn my head slowly and that smile and those eyes are on me. Caleb.

"What are you doing here?" I ask, my voice rising an octave or two.

"Well, I could say the same thing to you. I'm going home."

"Oh," I answer, "so am I."

He jumps over the seat to sit opposite me. He folds his arms and a tattoo flashes above the top of his shirt but, still fascinated by his chain, I ask, "What do you have around your neck?"

He gives me a vague look.

"I mean, what is on your chain?"

He pulls it out from beneath his shirt, raises the pendant to his lips and kisses it. "It's Maria Magdalena," he says with passion.

Was that an Italian accent?

"That's nice," I say. I don't want to ask about the tattoo, just in case it's some other religious icon. My desire for him suddenly wanes. Is it because he's wearing a Mary Magdalene medal around his neck or is it because he kissed it? I'm not sure. I pretend not to be interested in him and look out the window at the moving landscape outside the train. But his eyes are still on me. I can feel his gaze boring into my soul, even while he undresses me with his eyes.

"What do you write?"

"Excuse me?" I ask, forced to look at him. His face glistens with sweat, a golden sheen covering his olive complexion.

"What do you write?" he asks again, his eyes smiling at me. It's something so cheeky, so familiar and sexy, I can hardly breathe.

I feel the fire rise in my cheeks again and I stammer, "Ah, I write science fiction."

"Hmm, that's interesting. All futuristic kinda stuff, eh, like Star Wars?"

"I suppose."

He leans forward and places his hands on my knees. The heat of his body penetrates mine.

"What do you mean you suppose? You either do or you don't."

I look into his eyes, his face moves in closer, lust invading my space. His lips touch mine again. He presses hard and I press back. This is sheer lunacy, kissing a complete stranger on a train, yet I can't resist. His lips taste sweet and the smell of musk and sandal-wood fills my senses. He pulls away slowly, gently teasing and smiles, "So, what is it?"

"What?" I ask stupidly.

"What is it? Do you write Star Wars or not?"

Oh, shit, he's on about that again. How am I going to explain what I write? I don't want to discuss writing with him. He has me so distracted. "Actually, I don't write anything like that."

"Okay, so what kind of science fiction can it be?"

"Well, it's not."

"Well then," he asks teasingly, "what do you write?"

"Horror," I blurt out.

"Ah, so you write about me then?"

I frown with uncertainty as he leans forward again. His brow creases above his nose, his eyes darken and his breath quickens. Totally mesmer-ised, like under some type of spell, I ask, "What do you mean?"

My heart begins to race, a hint of fear spreads up my spine for the second time today.

His finger trails my arm, leaving goose bumps in its wake and he says, "Well, I relish writers, and their thoughts."

He leans even closer, his eyes growing darker, the heat intensifying, everything around me swirling. The nameless faces on the train are now empty voids of nothing. The landscape outside has darkened and all I can see is his eyes, his full lips and feel the fire emanating from his body as he moves closer. He presses his lips to my ear, sweeping his tongue down my neck then rising and nibbling my earlobe before whispering, "If you write horror, you must write about me."

My body sizzles as his lips find mine again. There was something about the way he kissed, his lips soft yet firm, wanting and teasing at the same time. I can't stand it anymore, my legs writhe with restlessness and my pelvis aches with a longing I have never experienced before. Finally, my body shakes with orgasmic relief.

His tongue continues to trace the line of my neck, then he buries his face into my breasts, placing gentle kisses upon my cleavage while he strokes my arms. My breath catches in my chest. Somewhere in the distance I can hear my voice, a tiny sound against the rhythmic clatter of the train saying, "I don't understand."

More warmth penetrates my ears and a whisper hangs there. "Give me something, just a sentence."

I smile, then giggle. "Who the fuck are you?"

"I'm the devil."

"Yeah, right and I'm your fallen angel."

"Excuse me, miss?" This voice is much louder. It startles me. I look around. Caleb is gone and in his place is a nameless face like all the others in the carriage. I look out the window. The landscape of suburban houses and barren backyards returns. I look back towards the voice. A man in uniform is waiting expectantly. "Do you have your ticket, miss?"

Bewildered and confused, I fumble in the top pocket of my jeans and pull out a screwed-up piece of paper. I hand it to the ticket inspector. He nods gratefully, passes it back and heads towards the end of the train. The man opposite me looks at me strangely. I feel flustered, but try not to show it. I quickly check myself and everything seems normal. The magazine is still in my lap, but words and sentences are flowing freely through my mind. I am alive with ideas. I patiently wait for my stop, keen to get home to write it all down.

"You're kidding me!" Kerri yelled above the noise of steady chatter and laughter of the crowded pub.

I smiled and said, "Nah, that's what happened, and you know what? After all those amazing ideas, do you think I could remember one of them when I got home?"

"Oh, my God! You need to get out more," Kerri said, kicking my foot affectionately, and smiling with a wicked glint in her eye.

"Whatdya mean? Just because you've been halfway around the world," I quipped.

"You were supposed to come with me, Lisa, but no! You had this bloody book to write."

"Yeah, well I'm trying."

"Well, you're not trying hard enough. Ever since I've been back all you tell me is how you can't write. You're too busy conjuring up men who don't exist, instead of just getting on with it."

Kerri punched me playfully in the arm and continued, "Just bloody well hurry up and get the damn thing written so you can come travelling with me."

"You've only just got back!"

"I know, but I think you need a rest from your imagination." Kerri raised her glass, took a large swallow then said, "If only Caleb were real, hey?"

I smiled knowingly at Kerri, leaned back in the vinyl clad booth, sipped on my Baileys and laughed, "Who says he's not real?"

CHILD SUPPORT

Kylie Chan

She sat on the couch in the living room and shuffled her notes. The spring breeze, full of the fragrance of frangipani and jasmine, billowed through the gauzy living room curtains. She stopped for a moment, enjoying the scent and the feeling of her long blonde hair being lifted by the warm air currents. A kookaburra laughed in the trees outside the house—rain coming.

Something different interrupted the floral fragrance—something faintly reminiscent of burning rubber. The kookaburra went silent. A large flock of crows landed in the gum tree outside her house and thrashed through the branches, cawing raucously.

The doorbell rang. She put her notes aside and rose to answer it.

He stood in the doorway and smiled slightly. Her heart twisted. Even after so many years, he still did it to her. Tall, bronzed, dark hair, dark eyes. Red and black and delicious. His smile grew slightly.

"Aren't you going to invite me in?"

She moved back and waved him inside.

"How're the kids?" he said.

"They're good. David has a tutor for physics, and his grades have improved. Penny had a sleepover last weekend, a few nice girls. I have photos, if you want to see."

He sat at the dining table and looked around. "I always loved this house." His voice was like velvet. "We built it together."

She flicked the kettle on and pulled two mugs out of the cupboard. "Tea or coffee?"

"Coffee." He didn't need to tell her he had it black.

She nodded. While she waited for the kettle to boil, she sat down at the table and picked at one of the placemats.

"How's the writing?" he said.

"It's coming along. You know how difficult it is to find a publisher, though. When it's finished, I'll have a battle."

"You know you don't need to fight for it if you don't want to. I can do it all for you."

She didn't reply.

"I'm glad you have something like this. Something interesting and creative." His voice became softer and even more silky. "Am I in it?"

"I think you're in everything. Being here is terrific. There's a large, active community of wonderful people."

"You're only here because you married me in the first place."

She tilted her head without looking up. "You may be right."

"If you had the chance, would you do it again?"

She rubbed her hands over the placemat.

"Do you need more child support, Ari? You shouldn't have to work if you don't want to. If you just want to write, you should be able to."

She glanced up into his eyes and was hypnotized. He smiled. She gasped and looked away. "Please."

"I'll arrange it." He reached across the table to touch her.

She shot to her feet and scurried to the kettle. "David's more expensive every year. He learns the guitar, he has a tutor, he eats like a horse. One more year of school, and then he has to decide what he wants to do, but if he goes to University here, it'll cost even more."

"I'll send you more, Ari. All you have to do is ask."

She dropped her head. The kettle whistled and she pulled it off the heat, then opened the cupboards to find the coffee.

"Tell me, Ari. Would you do it again, if you had the chance?"

She opened the coffee jar and hunted around in the drawer for a spoon.

"Instant," he said with scorn. "So where are they? I'm calling them, but only David's answering."

David loped out of the hallway and stopped. He strode to his father with his arms out. They embraced.

"Dad."

"David." He ruffled David's dark hair. "You'll be taller than me soon."

David snorted. "Not likely." He turned to speak to Ari. "I guess we can go."

"I want to see your sister first," he said.

"She's in her room, Nick. You want me to get her?"

Nick pulled David to sit next to him. "Sure. I'll make the coffee. You want coffee, David?"

"Nah, thanks, Dad, I don't like the taste."

Penny's room was pink and messy. She sat in the middle, eyes wide, clutching her well-worn teddy.

"Daddy wants to see you, darling."

"I don't want to."

"He won't hurt you, sweetheart; he loves you."

Penny shifted so that she faced away from her mother.

"He's your father, Penny. You need to see him. You don't have to go with him, you can just say hello."

Penny peered around her teddy. "I don't have to go?"

Ari crouched down and spoke gently. "No, sweetheart, you can stay here with me. David's visiting his father, but you don't have to. All he wants is to say hello."

"He wants to see me, doesn't he?"

"Yes, sweetheart."

Penny sighed. "He'll be sad if I don't say hello. It will hurt him if I don't say hello. I can say hello."

"Good girl." Ari held her hand out and Penny took it.

They returned to the dining room together. Nick and David sat laughing. Nick rose and held his arms out for Penny.

Penny hesitated, then straightened up and walked to her father.

He lifted her easily to sit on his hip. "Hello, darling."

She looked up at him, serious. "Hello, Daddy."

He moved his face close to hers. "Has your Mummy been saying bad things about me?"

She shook her head and her blonde braids flapped against her back. "No, Daddy. She's says you are what you are and you can't change it. But most of all, you love me and will never hurt me."

Nick glanced at Ari. "That's right." He gently lowered Penny. "Are you sure you don't want to come with me? We can have a lot of fun."

Penny backed to Ari and her eyes grew even wider.

"She's your daughter more than anything else, Ari."

Ari gestured towards David. "And he's your son." She glared at David. "Remember what I said. No involvement in the business until you're eighteen. You can watch if you have to, but you're strictly hands off. I don't want you making a decision about this until you're old enough."

David slumped, resigned. "Yeah, yeah, whatever." He put his hand out. "Come on Dad, let's go."

Nick grinned. "There's a red Ferrari parked out the front. How about we take that?"

"Way cool!" David shouted, his voice squeaking as it broke. He raced out the front door and slammed it shut behind him.

"Can I go back to my room, Mummy?"

Ari didn't look down. "Sure, Penny."

After she'd gone, Nick gazed into Ari's eyes. "Would you do it all again, Ari? They're fantastic kids."

"Sometimes they drive me completely nuts." She sat at the table and sipped the coffee. She frowned. He'd changed it. Instant wasn't good enough.

He sat across from her and smiled slightly. "I still love you, you know. I'd give it all up in a second and come back here to be with you."

"You are a selfish abusive bastard when I'm yours. You're a prince when I'm not. I'm not yours any more, Nick, and I never will be."

"Was it worth it, though?"

She looked down, trying to avoid his eyes.

"Ari," he said. "Ari, answer me. If you could do it all again, would you? We had some really good times. We have two wonderful children. It was a great life while it lasted."

She looked up again.

"Tell me the truth." He smiled and raised his hand. "No, of course you'll tell me the truth. If you could do it all again, would you? Would you still tear your wings off for me?"

She glanced away.

"It will hurt me if I never know the answer, Ari. You know you're incapable of hurting anyone. Tell me."

She nodded.

"That's all I needed to know. There's five hundred thousand dollars in the bank account, and you can keep the Ferrari. I love you, Ari, I always will, and any time you want me back, I'm yours."

"You can't help being what you are, Nick."

But he was already gone.

LAST NIGHT

Mark Curtis

"You want?"

Jess wiped the sweat streaming off her forehead as the man gestured into his shop a second time, unable to believe she was even thinking about it. She tore her eyes away from the flash in the tattoo parlour's window to check him out. He wasn't a Thai. He was too tall and his skin shone like polished anthracite. He might have been from North Africa, or India. Then her gaze returned to the image in the parlour's window that had caught her eye and imagination in the first place.

"What's that?" she finally asked, pointing to the sketch of a naked woman with a voluptuous figure, but the head of a crone. What really intrigued her was that it held a man's head by the hair. While macabre, it was also elemental. *And I can do with "elemental" in my life*, she thought. *Working hard and being professional has gotten me nowhere.* The bitterness over the reason for the sudden week's leave in Phuket sprung anew, and she looked enviously at the figure. *I wish I could do that to James. That would teach the bastard to steal stories and mouth off in the office.*

The shopkeeper looked at the flash, then back at her with respect.

"Kali. Great Goddess. Very powerful, very good luck. You come in, I draw picture again for you. You see, very safe, very clean."

Jess hesitated, looking around. The market was a dense knot of flesh, the grungier clothes of the tourists mixed with the colourful cottons of the native Thai. She wiped her brow again. The noon sun was blazing and the scents of cooking meat and coconut milk wafted throughout the market as hundreds of lunches roasted away. No one appeared to be taking any notice of her, but she felt like the centrepiece of a drama. Suddenly, the press of the bodies in the street and the heat felt oppressive. She looked back at the flash, then the darker womb of the shop.

The man gestured inside again with a smile. Dressed in calico pants and a white cotton shirt, his clothing contrasted sharply with his skin. She normally would never have even considered it, but after being accosted by all the panhandlers selling counterfeit clothes, watches and sunglasses, he was a welcome change. He had just been standing quietly in his doorway, patiently watching the crowd, while she gazed at the artwork in his window. Plus, she realised, he had a nice smile. Open and honest.

"No one know," he said, picking the last reason for her hesitation in an instant. "Secret." He paused for a moment, and then smiled again. "Our secret. Please, I draw this." He touched the sketch in the window quickly. "I draw carefully for you, then you choose."

Finally, Jess shrugged. She could go in and just have a look. At least in the parlour, she could decide in comfort, away from the prying eyes of the street and out of the heat.

"Okay."

She shook her backpack from her shoulder and stepped into the shop. It was delightfully cool after the heat outside, and she plucked at her shirt, trying to dry the sweat around her bra. The tattooist walked over to a small fridge and pulled out a jug of liquid and a tray of ice. Pouring a glass, he deftly added ice and offered it to her. She accepted cautiously, sniffing it to try and work out what it was.

"Juice," he said with another smile, pouring himself a glass and taking a sip.

Jess gave a nervous laugh and took a sip herself. It was delicious, the sweet taste of pineapple balanced the pleasant tang of lemon, with several other flavours swirling around. It refreshed her almost instantly, the heat of the day dropping away sharply.

"Five minutes, please. I draw picture for you," the tattooist said as he put the jug down and sat, picking up a clean sheet of paper and a pencil.

"Thank you," she said absently, studying the shop. Even though she would want it clean, she was surprised at just how spotless the parlour was. The needle gleamed inside a UV steriliser, like one she had seen in hairdressers' back home. In a sharp contrast to the rest of the market, there wasn't a speck of dirt anywhere. It was as if she was the first person who had set foot inside since it was built. The only thing out of the ordinary was that the same figure of the flash occupied a niche in the wall over the shopfront, caught in a dance pose.

"Unusual, yes?" the tattooist's voice broke her reverie.

"Sorry?" Jess said, startled to hear his voice.

"I worship Kali. Many other shrines in Phuket, mostly for Buddha, sometimes for Shiva, or Vishnu. Never Kali. But I know. *Know.*" His coal-black eyes burned with intensity. Jess shivered, the shop suddenly seeming colder, goosebumps breaking out on her arms. She could see why the figure was in the niche, unable to be seen from the street. His passionate intensity was at odds with the easy-going Buddhism she'd seen everywhere else in Phuket.

"The Goddess is greatest of all, because she is both creator and destroyer." He relaxed slightly, then smiled again, suddenly shy. "Here, this how it look when I finish," he said, reversing the flash with a flourish.

The image was similar to the one in the window, but reduced to only an inch or so high. Despite that, Jess immediately recognised it, impressed with the added detail. Now, the female was drawn boldly stepping forward, with the man's head swinging slightly. The action appealed immensely to Jess; one down, lots to go. *Places to be, men to behead.* She giggled at the thought.

"Very small," she finally said when she realised that he was waiting for her comment.

"It fit."

"Fit where?"

He smiled again, then slowly extended a finger to touch her right hip. "Here. No one see. Your secret."

Jess took another sip of the juice, the tension in her about going back to Brisbane tomorrow melting away. Jess, the office doormat, going nowhere, would have a tattoo that no one except her knew about. Of a Goddess who decapitated men. *Decapitate one, why not decapitate them all?* She giggled again.

"Yes?" he asked.

"Yes," she nodded.

He rose and closed the blinds on the shopfront, then pulled back a curtain to reveal a vinyl covered bench, which he then covered with a clean white sheet. He patted the bench in invitation, but raised a hand, stopping her as she dropped her backpack on the floor and moved towards it.

"Your clothes," he murmured, looking down at the floor.

Jess took another gulp of juice, then put the glass down. Normally shy, inhibition had deserted her. She casually slipped both her shorts and panties off, lying down on the bench.

She should have felt at least nervous when the hum of the needle started, but instead she felt serenely calm, detached from the world. A sharp pain surprised her when the tattooist started scribing, but then she saw the statue in the niche, looking down at her. The pain dropped away as she studied the intricately carved figure, taking in its powerful lines.

Afterwards, walking away from the parlour beneath the darkening sky, she didn't believe she had actually done it. A slight soreness at her hip where her panties and shorts rubbed against the skin was the only reminder. The pain was a distant memory. The tattooist had sung as he scribed, melodic and rhythmically calming her as the needle worked the flesh, adding detail after detail. Her only clear memory was the dancing figure, high in its niche, watching her as the tattooist went about his work.

When she got back to her room, she lifted her panties and the edge of the bandage to check it had really happened. Her skin was a bit raw, the area swollen and a rash surrounded the Goddess. But as she studied it, the figure became clearer, boldly striding into the future, ready for business. She looked at it closely, impressed even more with his skill. She could see why it had taken so long. He had added even more detail. The muscles in the figure's arms and abdomen were clearly defined, the head more haggish, with a slight suggestion of fangs.

She pressed the bandage back and eased her panties down. She thought about taking it easy and lying down, then discarded the idea. That was the old Jess thinking. It was time for a celebratory drink, after all it might be the last night of her holiday, but it was the first of the new Jess. She looked at herself in the mirror. Cautious doormats did not have a tattoo on their hip. Cautious Jess had asked James his opinion of her story idea. Doormat Jess had stayed silent, believing him when the prick had stolen it and said it would attract more attention under his by-line, and then two of them would share the glory.

She picked up her purse and room keys. That girl was dead, and caution was definitely out from here on. Now, she had dared and now she would win.

Halfway through the night's partying, she realised the tattooist had never asked for payment.

Jess stepped onto the train, the rush hour crowd reluctantly making way for her. Despite it being her first day back at work, she was in an excellent mood. The last night in Phuket, she had ended up fending off not one, but three gorgeous guys. She had delighted in dancing with all of them equally, keeping them guessing who would be the lucky one. The crestfallen looks as she kissed them all goodnight, then left, had been priceless. Just thinking about it still left a glow; nothing like that had happened to her before. And then on the flight home, one of the stewards had been especially attentive, plying her with drinks. Not even returning to the office, after the débâcle that saw her suddenly take a week's leave, could dim her mood.

She walked from Central Station to her office, enjoying the crispness of the Brisbane morning after the heat of Phuket. Walking through the door of the *Telegraph's* office, she even managed to smile, grabbing a coffee on her way to the desk. James was in his new office, talking on the phone and waving a fax around, looking harried.

Probably something to do with the Rollason story, she thought. She watched him for a moment, her sunny mood slipping away. Now she was reminded of the reason she had taken the holiday. He caught sight of her watching him, and stopped his tirade in mid-sentence. Inside the glass walls of his office, he reminded her of a lab rat in a tank. She gave him a cold smile and started reading her e-mail, scanning the correspondence generated during her leave. Halfway through, she came across a memo from personnel. She was being shifted out of Features to Advertising. From a reporter to a copywriter.

Her blood boiled instantly. She snapped a look at James, who now had his back to her and was waving out the window. *He did this to shut me up,* she thought as she crushed the memo and threw it in the bin. *Screwed three times over.*

Fuming at him, she scratched her hip, the skin responding with a tingle in return. The tattoo had been sensitive ever since getting back to Australia. She watched James pick up the phone and begin another tirade. Tirades were not unusual in his life, she mused, but two in quick succession indicated more stress than normal. Cold determination oiled through her, quashing her anger. Anger had made her simply walk out and take a holiday which, she realised, had been tacit admittance that James's claims over the authenticity of the story had been true. She wasn't going to blow her cool again; she was going to fight. And she was going to win. She checked the incoming fax tray; it hadn't been cleared yet.

Temptation briefly warred with her inherent caution. Deciding quickly, she rose and walked across the office. She casually reached out and cleared the entire tray, then returned to her desk. James was absorbed in his phone call, everyone else in their first cup of coffee or each other's stories of the weekend. Satisfied that no one had noticed, she studied the faxes. It took only thirty seconds before she found the reason for his stress.

The paper's lawyers had provided a one-page summary of where the *Telegraph* stood if a quoted source suddenly retracted what he had previously said was true. Jess leaned back in her chair, thinking rapidly. She knew what that meant. Rollason was going to withdraw as the "highly placed source" in the *Telegraph's* exposé on government corruption. With one feature out and two more to go, the *Telegraph* was going to be left floundering. James must be running around, looking for either another source, or a stick to bring Rollason back into line. She knew that there were no other sources. Rollason had so many weaknesses; there were a lot of sticks. The real question was: how to best use the information to her own advantage?

She saw the managing editor, Lawrence walk in, dapper as always. He smiled and waved distractedly at her on his way past. His wife's death had transformed his previous workaholic mentality into a vague shell that appeared in the mornings and vanished in the afternoons. Jess tapped a pencil as she thought. However, he had been at the helm of the *Telegraph* for over ten years, and its reputation was going to suffer severely if only one article of a three article expose was run, or even worse still, a retraction.

She got up and grabbed the incriminating correspondence. She crossed the office to Lawrence's door, pleased that his PA, Andrea, wasn't there. Lawrence was sipping tea, staring absently out the window. He started at the knock.

"Oh, Jess. How are you? Good holiday?"

"Fine, thanks, Mr Lawrence, but I thought you should see this." She strode around his desk and handed him the summary. "I believe Matthew Rollason is getting a lot of heat, and has said he won't continue as the inside source in the expose."

Lawrence looked at the fax, frowning. "But . . . ."

"Matthew Rollason is the source James is using for the series on the use of public monies for private interests in the Government."

Her words took several moments to register, then they impacted on him. "Christ. That story is the centrepiece of Saturday's edition for the next two weeks. James will have to get this sorted out damn quick."

"It was James who caused the problem," Jess answered quickly. "Matthew Rollason can be handled, believe me I know how. Really, I think you should be looking for a new solution to the problem, rather than just a band-aid fix."

Lawrence stiffened for a second, then leaned back in his seat "Oh, do you now? And why is that?"

"It was my story. James stole it, claiming it was his to get the associate editorship. But he would have never interviewed Rollason face to face, and he wouldn't have picked up on what a little rabbit the man is." She tapped the fax to emphasise the exposure the paper faced. "I know that bargaining would not be the way to handle him; you're better off grabbing his nuts and squeezing. And I know I can do a better job with this than James."

Lawrence looked up at her, merely tapping a pencil against his desk as she spoke. "Uh huh. I see where we are going with this conversation. Well, young lady, I applaud your ambition, but having just promoted James, I'm not going to turn around and ditch him. I'm quite sure that if James is properly motivated he can resolve the issue as well, and I'm not going to replace him just for this."

Jess's heart thudded. Not stroking Rollason before and after the first story appeared was such a huge mistake. Faced with the threat of him rolling over and collapsing, she had been sure Lawrence would replace James. Now she was badly exposed, with James certain to carry out his plan to have her shifted to Advertising. Lawrence continued looking at her, smiling slightly, but he was still negative. He might have lost interest in the *Telegraph* recently, but he still knew what was at stake. His silver hair caught the morning sun, a tinge of red shone briefly, a reminder of what once was.

He was not, Jess thought, an unattractive man, just temporarily lost. She was committed now. Either she brought him on side, or she was finished at the paper.

"John," she said softly, leaning closer. "I think you might be mistaken." She let her top gape, revealing the swell of her breasts, while placing her hand on his thigh. "To turn Rollason around will demand the right touch. I know him, because I was the one who separated him out from the herd of 'Yes' men the Premier has. If I bring him back on board, it will be a vindication of my claim that the story was mine to begin with, and proof that you saw through James's deceit. Not just that. I believe I am an excellent writer, and the expose is just the start of the stories I can hunt down. Surely, a win-win scenario for all those involved?"

Lawrence's eyes had widened at the contact from her hand, and he had opened his mouth to say something. Now both his eyes and mouth closed as she began stroking the top of his leg with her nails, moving slowly closer to the junction of his thighs.

"Bu . . . But the next story runs in five days. How are you going to convince Rollason to stay on board as the pressure gets even stronger?" he gasped.

She leaned even closer, her lips close to his ear, her nails reaching his fly. "John, I can be very persuasive when I need to be. Perhaps we can meet after work and I can explain my plans further?"

Shivering, he nodded rapidly. "Of course. Of course. There's no harm in talking further."

She dropped her voice to the barest whisper, stroking him openly. "Call James in after I leave, and inform him of the consequences of his actions. Then leave the rest up to me. I promise you, financially and personally, you won't regret it."

Jess heard the distant sound of a file hitting the desktop outside. The door was ajar and, through it, she saw Andrea's normally prunish face stretched in surprise at the scene inside. Some peripheral damage control would be required there, Jess thought quickly, then returned her attention to the main target.

Jess gave him one long stoke, producing a gasp of pleasure, then smiled and stood up.

"So I'll see you tonight, then. Say at seven, somewhere out of the way?"

Breathing hard, he nodded again. "Yes, yes. Good idea."

"O'Reilly's then. At seven. I'll leave you to your work."

Calmly, Jess walked out, firmly closing the door behind her. Andrea had inflated herself like a balloon, Cerberus crossed with Hitler, ready to deal out a reprimand. But she was only a PA, and Jess would soon control Lawrence. Andrea just had to be informed of the new pecking order.

"John will need a few minutes before you go in, Andrea," Jess said, standing casually in front of his door.

"His name is Mr. Lawrence to you, girl. What do you think you were doing in there?" Andrea demanded.

"None of your business. You know," Jess leaned in to whisper confidentially to her, "you really shouldn't purse your lips like that, Andrea. Somewhere, a cat's now lost its arse. The RSPCA will be after you in no time."

For a second, the other woman's face froze, then went deep red.

"How dare you! I will only ask you once more. What were you doing?

"Nothing that concerns you."

"It certainly looked like *something*."

"If you really think so, ask John yourself," Jess replied, smiling at her. She steadily regarded Andrea, until the other woman finally looked away. "But like I said, you should give him a few minutes before you go in."

With that, she turned and walked to her desk, grabbing her purse. Her hip itched and she lightly touched it through the skirt, hoping it hadn't got infected. On the way out, she smiled sweetly at James, who suddenly froze mid-tirade. She was laughing to herself by the time she got to the elevators. She would grab a muffin at the foodcourt; she needed to be out of the office for the next act.

Down on Queen St, the morning's crispness was giving way to a pleasant warmth. Briefly basking in the sun as she emerged from the building, she strolled down to Anzac Square, descending the circular stairs to the underground foodcourt. Sitting outside the bakery, she had taken just two bites out of her muffin, when she felt a hand grab her shoulder.

"You fucking *bitch*," James spat in her ear.

Calmly, she turned to face him. "Good morning, James, have a good weekend?"

"Don't you act coy with me, you meddling little cow. Lawrence just told me he's handing you an associate editorship, and control of Saturday's crime feature. You must be out of your fucking mind. There's no way you'll be able to handle it."

"Let's not air our dirty knickers in public, James. Follow me." Jess rose and walked through the eastern gap in the foodcourt's shopfronts. She turned at the elevators and approached the double door that led out to the loading docks. The door should have only opened one-way into the foodcourt, but things like that were no longer an obstacle. In a sharp contrast to the gleaming foodcourt, the dock was battered and grimy. Dried shreds of foodstuffs littered the wide hallway that led out to the actual receivals dock where the trucks pulled in. At this time of the morning, it was totally deserted. The two of them moved out of the echoing corridor and came to a halt near the lip of the dock.

"Now, James, what seems to be the problem?" She kept her tone aggravatingly sweet, hoping to incite him further. It worked, the veins in his neck beginning to stand out and his fists clenching at his side.

"Andrea told me you'd been in to see Lawrence, and that you had your hand in his crotch. You must be out of your tiny mind if you think fucking Lawrence is going to get you anywhere."

"Why won't fucking get me anywhere, James? Fucking me, then fucking me over got you the story and a promotion. And you're as thick as two short planks and lousy in bed. Imagine where it's going to get me?"

His face flushing an even deeper red, James stepped closer to her. "High and mighty little tart." His finger stabbed into her shoulder, emphasising the last word of the sentence. "Jumped up little bitch." Stab. "I am going to fuck you," stab, "and the paper so badly, you will beg me," stab, "for help."

He stood over her, his eyeballs red from last night's booze, his breath reeking of coffee. Behind him, a truck appeared in the adjacent laneway, its engine reverberating in the concrete surrounds, its beeper sounding the alarm as it backed down the narrow dock.

"James," she quietly told him, "you are so wrong."

With that, her hands hammered upwards, deep into his chest. The force of the blow crushed his ribcage and lifted him clear over the lip of the dock. He hit to unforgiving concrete with a wet smack. The first the driver knew of his arrival was the bump he made under the truck's wheels.

Before the brakes even screeched, Jess was back inside the foodcourt, her hip itching madly. Walking casually, she made her way down to the toilets. Luckily, they were empty and she stopped in front of the vanity, lifting her skirt to check her hip in the mirror. To her surprise, the tattoo was flushed with blood. She touched it tentatively, expecting pain. But the skin only tingled. She lightly scratched it, and the sensation grew into a pulse of pleasure, travelling to her groin, then fading. As she studied the tattoo closer, she realised that the man's head had light drops of blood outlined. Then the hag's head, ever so slightly, turned to regard her in the mirror, and inclined in acknowledgment of her efforts so far, before resuming its stance.

She let her skirt drop and smoothed it down, then absently scratched her hip yet again. She smiled at the powerful throb the action provoked.

"I can get used to that," she announced, looking at herself in the mirror. First she had to pay Rollason a little visit, then she had to finish the story. And from now on, she realised, she'd have to write like hell.

VIVA LA REVOLUTION!

E. Robert Dobson

Though the office's incandescent spots had been turned down tonight, there was enough light cast from the monitor and television. His face painted pale and overlaid with cathode explosions, Mark caressed the keyboard, the rhythmic plastic clicking soon underscoring a disembodied monotone voice. "Testing. Testing. This is a synch test. Is everything cool?"

Mark looked across from his monitor to the TV in front of his desk. The live feed from the studio had kicked in and Ash, the sound guy, was slumped in the host's chair, going through his nightly routine of tests and calibrations. Mark picked up the remote control and muted the TV. Turning back to the computer, he looked at the start he'd made on his resumé. He didn't want to write it any more. He shouldn't have to write it anymore. *Late Link* was a great show to work for and, frankly, if he didn't have to go he wouldn't. The problem was the network had hammocked the show's three month series run between reality TV show feeds and the Christmas holiday ratings slump. Unable to contemplate the future, Mark switched documents to tonight's notes for Ed Hartley, the show's host, who was responsible for stringing together an hour and a half of repackaged clips of Italian housewives stripping, insanely violent Japanese game shows and cruelly redubbed telenovellas. For a moment, he considered dropping the joke about the Kangaroo Point tunnel worker's strike but decided against it. Even though he was a lefty at heart the situation there was too strange not to be derided in some way.

Mark printed the document and passed it on to a harried assistant as he left. The heavy security door swung shut behind him as Mark walked out into the balmy night air. From between the trees, he could see the lights of Brisbane spread out around him. It had been raining and light wisps of steam rose from the asphalt.

Starting up his beat up old Mazda hatchback, he took the long way down Mt Cootha, along the ridge top and down the winding forested roads. He was trying to decide whether he should take the Bardon turnoff when it happened. The lights went out all over the city. The world became silent. He slammed on the brakes, found they weren't working fast enough, then wrenched the handbrake on. Gravel crunched beneath the wheels as the car swerved off the road. Mark swung the steering wheel, trying to correct the car's direction, but it only made things worse. There was a thud as he hit something in the darkness. The car spun around and, much to Mark's relief, came to a sudden stop.

For a moment the only sound was distant traffic, but then there was a voice.

"Sorry about that," the voice said in a rather polite and gentlemanly tone, "but I didn't want to miss you."

"Who are you?" Mark replied as he got out of the car. Looking around, he was unable to see anybody in the gloom. A dim light shone over Mark's left shoulder and he spun around to see a man sitting cross-legged on top of his car.

"Jesus fucking Christ!" Mark recoiled back.

The man on the car wore a black suit and had a goatee of the type that was oh-so-hip if you lived in Seattle and it happened to be 1994. He smiled at Mark, then said, "Not quite. You can call me Ahriman."

"Huh?" Mark's mind didn't know where to start. He started looking for places to run, but he could barely see a thing beyond the car. The man stood up and the dim light surrounding him intensified slightly.

"I've come to offer you a job, Mark," Ahriman said, jumping off the car. Mark took another step back, but Ahriman made up the distance quickly. "It's a job I think you will like," he said.

"What type of job?" Mark stuttered.

"A writing job," the man replied. "My company is starting up in town and we're hiring. I think you have the skills to help us out."

The light around Ahriman was beginning to get quite bright.

"Look, perhaps this isn't the best time to discuss this," Mark said.

"Perhaps," Ahriman said, as he walked to the back of Mark's car, "but I think you'll appreciate what we are doing. We're committed to change, Mark, and what we do today will enhance everyone's lives from now on."

Mark didn't ask the question: What will he do today? He didn't want to know, best he just turn and walk away. "Look, I'm really ... " he began.

There was the screech of tearing metal as Ahriman ripped a palm-sized section off the back of Mark's car.

"Fuck! How the fuck ... " Mark blurted out, before realizing he shouldn't be doing anything to antagonize someone who can tear metal with their bare hands.

Ahriman held up the piece of metal. Affixed to it was the manufacturer's badge. He studied it a while, before pocketing it.

"It's a sign, it just has to be," Ahriman whispered.

Mark began praying, "Hail Mary, blessed be thy ... shit! Our father who aren't in ... no, art in heaven ... oh, god!"

Ahriman turned to Mark and said, "He won't help you, but, hey, in my defense I have been severely misrepresented. I'm not the person you think I am."

"You're the devil," Mark said.

"Uh huh," he replied.

"This job wouldn't happen to involve tempting me into selling my soul to you," Mark said, almost surprised by how brave he was, staring down the devil. It occurred to him that if he could outwit the devil he would be like a hero in a bluegrass song.

"Nope," the devil replied.

"What?"

"I already have your soul," the devil said. "And, like, I need to tempt you. You're doing a pretty good job of giving into temptation without my help."

Mark stumbled. He felt a sudden hollowness, a sickness in his stomach. He steadied himself against the side of the car and said, as a matter of fact, "I didn't believe in God and now I pay the price."

The devil laughed, "God has nothing to do with it. It's just . . . It's just the way of things. Almost everyone ends up in hell."

"Really?"

"No kidding. I'm running a census at the moment to figure out who actually got into heaven. Seriously, it's doing my head in. I have no idea what game the big feller is playing."

"So you don't eternally torment people?"

"I figure people do a good enough job of tormenting each other. I'm really superfluous to requirements in that regard."

"So what do you want from me?" Mark asked. A set of headlights wound their way around a nearby corner. Mark shielded his eyes from the glare. Ahriman didn't say a word as a black sedan pulled up beside them. The passenger door opened and a voice said: "Get in."

Mark looked into the vehicle to see Ahriman driving. Quickly spinning round, he saw the other Ahriman standing beside him. The one inside the car said, "I exist in 666 places at once. It's one of the perks of being El Diablo."

He motioned for Mark to get inside.

"What about bad people?" Mark asked when they had reached the Riverside Expressway. "What about Hitler or Stalin—surely you had to punish them?"

"I try to avoid playing God's game wherever possible," the devil replied as he lazily wove the car through traffic, "but some people need to understand actions have consequences, so I ended up instituting a system where everyone gets a chance to kick people like them in the crotch."

"A kick in the crotch?"

"Almost everyone is in hell," Ahriman reminded him. "It'll make your eyes water, trust me on this one."

"So I could kick Hitler in the nuts?" he asked.

"It's not mandatory," the devil replied, "but if you wanted to, then the opportunity does exist."

"What about the people who died before Hitler was born, why should they care?"

The devil shrugged. "I've found if you give someone the opportunity to kick some guy in the balls usually they'll take it. It's one of those wacky quirks of human nature."

The car had peeled off the expressway and was now navigating the narrow back streets of Kangaroo Point. It pulled up at a gateway in a wire mesh fence. Hessian fabric was tacked all over the fence to prevent people from looking inside. Mark recognized the place. They were at the tunnel site where the striking workers had barricaded themselves in for the past three weeks. The gates opened and Ahriman's car slipped inside.

Bright lights lit the sparse worksite. A few demountable offices and several shipping crates could be seen here and there. They stopped near the tunnel mouth and Mark, following Ahriman's lead, stepped out into the cool air that rose from the river.

"Is this your doing?" Mark asked. "The strike, I mean?"

"Kind of," Ahriman replied. "Though the workers choose to strike, they think it might buy me some time."

"Some time for what?"

"To reduce panic and to create an environment for a calm transition," the devil said. "But come now, follow me."

The path into the tunnel was well lit and wide, the bare earth compacted solid. A short way into the tunnel, they came across a group of workers gathered around a set of blueprints. Ahriman gave them a wave as he walked past.

"How's it going, boss? Found another convert, have we?" one of the men said. The devil laughed and replied, "I'm about to."

The pair walked down the tunnel for another thirty seconds before Mark saw it. Shimmering. Glowing. As he got closer he realized it took up the entire width of the tunnel. Through the pulsing waves of light, he could make out an image of what seemed to be a landscape of gentle hills and, nestled among them, a quaint village.

"This is a gateway, isn't it?"

"That it is," the devil replied. "Technically it's a gateway to hell, but I have real problems with the connotations that dredges up. We need to spin it a bit more, make it sound positive."

"It is though?"

"It is what?"

"Positive?"

"Oh, most certainly," the devil replied. "Yes, indeed. I'm unilaterally instituting a fundamental paradigm shift in the way realms interact, but this isn't a power play. If it stirs him up, well that's great. I'm not sure if it will though, but it's definitely time for changes."

"What sort of changes?" Mark asked.

"Well religion for one. Everyone fears death and some people follow rules in the vain hope of eternal salvation. Let's just say there are a lot of really bitter Christians in hell."

"You'd think they'd be happy with a relatively normal afterlife," Mark replied.

"You'd think so," the devil said, before asking, "You want to go through?"

Mark looked at the massive pulsating wall of energy in front of him and asked the devil, "You sure it's safe?"

"Pretty sure," the devil replied. "Besides, the worst thing that can happen is you die and go to hell."

The devil walked a few steps, slipping into the wall of energy. Mark closed his eyes and followed. When he opened them it was daylight. Lush green low hills spread as far as the eye could see. Nearby was the tiny village he'd seen. It was straight from a Victorian children's book. The devil smiled and gestured towards the landscape.

"See, here is the problem," he said. "Hell is infinite as far as I can tell. With unlimited resources no one wants for anything. Pretty much what you can imagine on earth can be found in hell."

"That doesn't sound like a problem," Mark replied.

The devil continued: "Apart from myself and the daemons, which are really just . . . no, it's too hard to explain . . . let's just say no one has any real power over you in hell."

"And?"

"You can't be threatened with death, you can't be bribed. You are who you are. Apart from me, everyone is equal and everyone shares equally. Some people are threatened by that concept."

"An open doorway would collapse the world economy. Godless communism would destroy capitalism—shit, just about any 'ism,'" Mark said.

"Hell is one of the few places Marxism has actually worked," the devil replied. "I'm quite proud of that. Still I don't want to cause any unnecessary suffering because of it."

He turned to Mark, placed a hand on his shoulder and said, "That's why I need people like you. Communicators, people who can inform the public about what's going on. So are you up for it?"

As Mark pondered his response, a family of four walked through the gate—a rough-as-guts middle-aged man in dirty overalls and his wide-eyed wife and kids.

"Comrade Diablo," the man said jokingly to the devil.

"Good to see you, Pat," the devil replied. "Nice to see the wife and kids too. Where are you off to?"

"Gonna take the kids to see grandpa and grandma and then I thought we'd finish off by kicking Hitler in the nuts."

"Be careful," the devil said, "the Hitler line can get pretty long towards the evening."

"I'll look out for that," the man replied. As he directed his family down the hill, he shouted out, "Viva El Diablo! Viva la revolution!"

The devil chuckled. "Some people just take to it. It's amazing, isn't it?"

"I guess so," Mark replied.

The devil stroked his beard and said, "How about you take tomorrow off, catch up with dead relatives—if you want something just ask someone to make it for you—then on Wednesday we can knock out some press releases before the great unveiling next week."

Mark spoke nervously as he replied, "This is essentially a demonic totalitarian state we're talking about—I'm not sure I can do this for you."

"You have moral concerns?" the devil asked, raising an eyebrow.

"Huh?" Mark was confused. Why would he be concerned really? No more hunger, no more fear and above all no more writing goddamned resumes. This was a ground floor opportunity in an organization with massive growth potential. Only a fool would deny this offer.

"No," Mark added. "I mean a week's not enough time for this job. At the least, we really need to be layering the information releases, so by the time people get the whole picture they're cool with it."

The devil grinned as he nodded his head, "Interesting idea, tell me more."

"See, hell, and communism, have a lot of negative

connotations . . . " Mark started to explain. In the distance, a quaint old train pulled up at the village. He would see what existed in that vast forever soon enough, but for now he was happy to be standing on the edge of hell discussing marketing theory with the devil.

AN HOUR WITH THE DEVIL

Lee Dublin

I wasn't that surprised to find His office was extremely stylish or that the chair in which I was invited to sit was deeply comfortable.

"Thanks for seeing me," I said nervously.

"Not at all," said the Devil. His smile was an attempt to put me at ease. "I'm never too busy to see a new client."

"Potential client," I was quick to say.

He nodded. "Of course." He gestured at my bag with its pitiful burden. "May I?"

As I passed my manuscript over the desk, I felt my apprehension return. He seemed to sense it immediately.

"Until you sign on the dotted line, my dear, nothing is binding."

I sighed, relieved, but a little embarrassed to be acting so awkwardly. The Devil lifted my draft manuscript in one hand, weighing it. He raised an eyebrow.

"Not bad," He said, but His tone was more honest than kind. He ran his thumb over the page edges, the text passing in a blur. "Choppy," He remarked. "Too many adverbs, possibly . . . "

I blushed. My shoulders hunched as I tried to make myself appear small. "It's only a first draft."

The Devil laid my papers on His desk and leaned forward, looking me in the eye. "Why did you come here today?"

I admit I hesitated. "I . . . I *really* do want to be a writer," I said. "I think."

"Ah." The Devil leaned back in His chair, an overlarge executive model with shining leather upholstery. "What's stopping you?"

I'd asked myself the same question time and time again. The yearning to write is always there, stories are a constant feature of my thoughts. When I am forced to do other things—work, spend time with family, complete chores—the desire to be at my keyboard, to be in my stories, is overwhelming.

Why then, when time is my own, do I find myself elsewhere? Reading a book; watching telly; looking at my fish tank. What is wrong with me? I took a deep breath. "I love writing, but maybe I don't love it enough to be a writer?"

The Devil steepled His fingers and gave me an indulgent smile. "Go on," He said.

I grimaced. My face was hot. "If I was meant to be a writer, wouldn't I find it easier? I mean, wouldn't I write every chance I got?"

"Perhaps." He tapped my manuscript with one long, immaculately manicured finger. "You *have* written this."

"A draft," I said, dismissing my work at once. "An attempt; it's taken me two years already. It's choppy—you said so yourself."

The Devil made a noise of agreement.

I went on. "It's not original. It's not very skilled. I can't find the words I want. The scenes . . . the plot is full of holes . . . "

"Stop." His voice was soft but commanding. "What do you want from me?"

I stared at Him, remembering where I was and who I was talking to. His easy smile was no longer apparent. His patient manner was gone. I was struck dumb. He stood and walked to the window of His office. Red-gold light, much like that of a sunset, lit His elegant features. Too late, I tried to stop my mind conjuring up the obvious thought: *hand-some devil*. The words flashed in my brain, scarlet neon cursive script. A pointed tail appeared as a flourish on the final letter.

"Alright," He said. The image in my mind vanished in flames and smoke. "You want me to fill you with passion for writing. You want the standard package: inspiration, originality, drive and a faster typing speed. I can do it. I'll even throw in the fame and fortune pamper pack." He turned to face me. "I'm right, yes?"

The expression on my face was not what He had been expecting. "Well," He demanded. "What do you want?"

I rose from the chair; it no longer felt as comfortable as it had when I'd first entered His office. "I want you to stop interfering," I said.

"What?"

Although I saw real menace in His eyes, my determination grew. "You know what I'm talking about: TV reality shows, computer games, beautiful sunny days when it's impossible to stay indoors!"

The Devil's astonishment transformed into an evil grin. "Onto me are you?" He folded His arms. "Well, my standard non-temptation package is a bit more costly. See, you're spoiling my fun."

I felt deflated, my shoulders slumped. "Tell me," I said.

He did. By the end, my red face had cooled—I guessed I was as white as good-quality paper.

"Well?"

I looked up. The Devil had returned to His desk. Seated on the edge, He was holding a pen in one hand and a thick sheaf of paper in the other.

"Um." I shuffled my feet and, feeling my legs trembling, sat down again. "How much to win the lottery so I can give up work instead?"

THE DEVIL BEHIND THE LOUVRES

Grace Dugan

The clearest, most memorable feature of art is how it arises, and the world's best works, in telling of the most diverse things, are in fact narrations of their own birth—BORIS PASTERNAK.

He stepped towards her, and suddenly his mouth was on hers.

No. That was no good.

The kiss was unexpected, but warm, and it filled her body with an ache.

No. No good. Delete.

In the act of kissing, which was so unexpected, it was as if they merged into one being.

Delete.

His lips captured hers, in a vice-like grip that was at the same time tender and urgent.

Ugh. Definitely delete that one.

Get a cup of tea. Tea is good. Helps you think. Caffeine is good. Wait for the kettle to boil, try not to think of the scene. Sit down at the computer and try again.

His lips were soft. His hands on her waist were warm, rough.

Ugh! Ugh! Ugh! Of course, his lips were soft. Well, not of course. What about:

He kissed her, hard, and it was like the crashing waves of the sea.

Nope. No good.

This is not working.

You look at the pile of manuscript on the desk, now maybe three centimetres thick. You run your hand over the top of it, lovingly. You can't stop now, you've only written eight hundred and seventy-two words today. You can't stop until fifteen hundred, or it will look bad on your chart on the wall, like a dud day, a day in which nothing was accomplished, a day which cannot justify itself.

And this is an important scene, the landing in the middle of the stairs, the turning point in the book.

You let yourself vague out. You stare at the map stuck up on your wall, a map of your world. You stare at the character descriptions, at the arranged and rearranged index cards of the plot.

What does the little book of *Creative Wisdom for Writers* say? You open it to a random page:

The desire for safety stands against every great and noble enterprise—TACITUS

You open it again.

You will get what you want if you work hard and don't die first—ZEN SAYING.

You close the book. You sit down at the computer again. You stare at the blue weatherboard wall of the neighbours' house. The louvres of their bathroom window are right opposite you, but a little higher, because their house is higher set than yours.

You lie on the bed and close your eyes. You try to imagine the scene. The hero, Joren, is standing there in his tunic, on the balcony of the castle. The protagonist, Merena, is standing near him, and they are talking, exchanging banter, and then they kiss. Why should that be so hard?

You imagine it is Fred, with whom you are infatuated. Fred looks strange in a tunic and with a sword on his hip, but kind of cute. His face moves towards yours. His lips are almost touching yours. He's kissing you. It feels good.

What are the words to describe this?

You open your eyes. The louvres are open, and the devil is watching you from the neighbours' bathroom.

You close the window. And lock it.

You get a bunch of books off your shelves, ones which have memorable kissing sequences in them. You go through them, find the page where the kiss is described, then laboriously copy it out into a notebook. People say it's good to copy out good writing; it makes you pay attention to how it's done. You look for similarities, differences, try to figure out what the clichés are, try to figure out how to make it new.

This all takes about two hours. Halfway through, you go to the toilet. When you walk into the bathroom, the devil is standing at the neighbours' kitchen window. This is the other neighbours. Their house is a little bit further away, maybe three metres, but level with yours, and he looks straight across at you.

"Hi," he says.

You smile, embarrassed. Of course, the devil would be able to go from one house to another. It's not like he would have to take out a lease. But, even if you know your neighbours, they're not supposed to say "Hi" to you unless you're out the front of the house.

He is young, and kind of scruffy. He has short hair, but looks as if he's once been a feral. He has a pretty serious tan. His horns are small and shiny, as if they're made of red lamé.

You close the curtain, and sit down on the toilet. It's embarrassing to think he's probably listening to you.

When you're washing your hands, you think about opening the curtain to see if he's still standing there. But if you do, you'll come face to face with him, and it will lack subtlety.

You sit on the back deck with your notebook and read through the kissing sequences you've copied out. You read them aloud, but under your breath, so the neighbours won't think you're talking to yourself. The devil starts playing the guitar and singing. He starts with Hendrix and works his way through the Rolling Stones to the Chili Peppers. His voice is strident, but a bit flat. You turn your head just a little and see him sitting on the neighbours' deck, under the umbrella with the little mirror ball tied to it.

He is really belting it out.

You go inside. You should do some housework. In her book, *Dear Writer*, Carmel Bird says it's a good idea to give up the housework if you want to become a writer. You think this is all very well, but it's really not a matter of giving it up, it's a matter of prioritising. And you find housework kind of calming, and sometimes inspiring, so you get out the vacuum cleaner and go over the rugs in the living room and in your bedroom.

It's not very inspirational.

You get out the blue bucket from the cupboard, fill it from the tap in the bath, and start mopping the kitchen floor. There is a clomping on the back stairs and the devil appears at the back door. He's wearing cargo shorts and a black Chesty Bonds singlet.

"Hey," he says, and walks right through your wet kitchen, across your vacuumed carpet and out to the front deck. He sits down on the old green couch and pulls a pack of cigarettes out of one of his cargo pockets.

You walk to the front door and stand there, mop in hand, looking at him with an expression which you hope will force him to explain himself.

"Have you got a light?" he asks.

"No," you say in a voice that is hopefully indignant enough to have some effect.

"That's a shame."

"Yeah, I guess it is." Sudsy water drips from the mop onto the deck. "Oh, well."

You stare at him in a manner calculated to make him feel uncomfortable. It doesn't seem to work.

"Can I ask you what you're doing in my house?" you say.

"Do you own this place? Really? I thought you were just renting it. If you own it, I'd be worried about that crack in the front wall. The whole place is going to collapse soon if you don't have that seen to."

"We are renting. It's still my house."

"Well, it's a house that you're renting. You having a lease on the house, doesn't exactly make it yours." He rolls a cigarette back and forth between his thumb and forefinger. "Are you sure you don't have a light?"

"Yes. Sure." You sigh, in heavy exasperation. "What are you doing here?"

"Oh, just passing through."

You sigh even more pointedly. You go back inside the house, lock the door between the house and the deck, and continue mopping. The devil has put dirty footprints on the kitchen lino, and now they've dried on, so you have to start again. He's also put dust on the carpet.

You are halfway through mopping the floor again and he appears at the back door and walks in.

"Here we go," he says with some enthusiasm. He walks up to the stove and pulls the stove-lighter off its nail. "You told me you didn't have a light!"

He lights his cigarette, puts the stove-lighter back on its nail, leans back against the window sill and smokes enthusiastically.

"Why did you lie to me?" he asks.

You stare at him, then you start mopping up his footsteps.

"I mean, really, I want to know."

"That's not really a lighter, anyway. It's not a cigarette lighter, it's for the stove."

He laughs, and it's a nice kind of laugh. "Yeah, but look!" He holds up the cigarette, waves it around.

"You shouldn't be smoking inside, anyway," you say. "We never smoke in the house."

"You never smoke at all."

"None of our friends ever smoke in the house. They sit out on the deck."

"But I'm not one of your friends."

You sigh again. "No, you're not." You put one hand on the mop and one on your hip and say, "What do you want?"

"What makes you think I want something?"

"Your manner."

He laughs.

"Come over here." He jerks his head in a beckoning way. His horns shine in the sunlight coming through the window.

You put down the mop and walk over to him.

"I'll tell you," he says, "but you should know that it's a secret."

"Unh-ha."

He leans towards you conspiratorially.

"You see, the thing is," he says, but then his arm is around you and he kisses you.

You keep thinking of fire and brimstone, but really he just tastes like cigarette smoke. Surely kissing the devil should be interesting, but this is really quite ordinary. In fact, he's a terrible kisser.

But that's just the way things are sometimes.

THE AGREEMENT

Paul Garrety

"Moonbeams are slippery suckers. Can't catch 'em. Like those little silver fish back home. So still, until you try to net them." He nodded, agreeing with himself, as always, then overbalanced with the movement. Hastily, he grabbed onto a tree branch to steady himself.

"His balance is sloshed with bourbon," he shouted across the river, words skimming like stones on the moonlit corrugations. "Can I say that?" Then, more loudly, "Can I say that?"

He turned away. He could say anything. He was a writer. But a writer with little more to say.

He awoke the next morning with the usual symptoms: headache, gummy mouth and a raging thirst. When does aberration become normal? When did a few dry writing days become an idea drought? When did an occasional few drinks become too frequent and too many?

Coffee. He flicked on the percolator that the housekeeper always left ready for him, remembering a time not that long ago when coffee just came in instant, odourless spoonfuls. Drunk for effect. Now, there's a snappy title for a book, he thought.

At least he wasn't broke, not yet. However, the advance for the third book was disappearing faster than last night's Jack D. How would he ever be able to give up this apartment? He carried his coffee out onto the balcony and looked up the river towards Toowong—so close to the city, such an easy stroll to his favourite pub, the Regatta . . .

The phone started ringing. Reluctantly, he went back inside.

"Peter! Darling, how are you?"

Shit. Barbara. He was sick of excuses. "Barbara, do all agents sound so cheerful at sunrise, or did I just luck out with you?"

"I guess that answers my first question. It's past ten where I live, sunshine," she said, her sandpaper voice coarsening a grade.

"Before you start again, Babs. I can't do this. I've spent nearly all their money. My pump is full on, but it's sucking air, and I've got a hangover that could quite possibly prove fatal, so I'm going to hang up now. Sorry."

"Wait. Peter . . . "

Her voice disappeared with a clunk. At least he felt better not lying anymore. The unfinished novel was like a growing pile of dog shit between them, both of them saw it, smelt it, but refused to acknowledge it. Well, this morning, he'd not only acknowledged it, he'd jumped right in the middle with bare feet and wriggly toes, and he felt better because of it. He noticed a crumpled business card lying beside the phone. Idly, he picked it up.

Has your muse deserted you?
Maybe you've just misplaced your creative spark?
We CAN help.
Ring Samuel A. Tan
The Ideas Factory

Where the hell had he picked that up? If only it were that easy. He flipped it back onto the table and went in search of more coffee.

The rest of the day was filled with finding excuses not to. Not to write, not to sit down in his office, not to confront the slimy-slow, gut-curling fear of having used it all up—the thought of never again being able to plug into the zone and feel the surge as worlds and people layered up, like digital pixels, a key stroke at a time.

When it got too much, he went out, driving fast down the hill towards the city, pretending to be going somewhere, aware he was escaping and hating himself for it.

At least the headache had gone.

Maybe he'd have lunch? Janet was always on at him to take her out during the day. Why not? He would take her to *Pier Nine*. At least he wouldn't be able to hear her chatter above the noise there. Afterwards, they could go back to her place. Maybe he'd even spend the night for a change. Anything but face that blinking, taunting cursor on his laptop. He reached for the mobile phone. It slipped from his fingers, bouncing onto the floor. He cursed. Keeping one hand on the wheel, he stretched across the front of the car. His fingertip brushed the phone. It slid out of reach a little more . . . .

The spin started slowly. When he bolted up from beneath the dashboard, it was too late. The Commodore that he'd slewed into was veering away; Peter's slow motion screeching slide towards the opposing lane of traffic was already underway.

"Are you all right?"

Peter looked up with a start. He tasted blood; his mouth was full of it. He swallowed and gagged. There was a lot of blood! What the hell had happened?

He must be dead, he decided; he had seen the traffic, a semi trailer, coming directly at him.

"You went right through a gap in the traffic, like Moses parting the Red Sea. You slid straight into this vacant parking space. Quite a tight fit it was too, if I don't say so myself. Here, let me help you out."

The voice sounded English. The car door opened. Peter felt strong hands beneath his arms. No one else was stopping. No one was even looking.

"Am I dead?" he asked, his voice rising, a feeling of dread coming over him. "Why isn't anyone taking any notice of what happened?"

The man touched Peter on the arm. The panic subsided. It was like a double hit of intravenous valium. He felt himself being guided into one of the shops and settled into a chair. An ornately framed mirror on the opposite wall reflected the gold lettering painted across the shop's plate glass window: *The Ideas Shop*.

"How?" he shook his head, mouth gaping.

The other man leant back against the wall, arms folded, a sardonic smile tugging at one corner of his mouth. He shrugged.

"I had to get you to stop somehow. You took no notice of the business card. No, don't say anything."

Peter tried to move, but felt as if he'd physically bonded with the chair. His head felt as if it was full of cotton wool, but he could still think, even if he couldn't move.

"I would have thought that after the dry patch you've been going through, Peter, the business card would have been enough, but for once it appears I was mistaken."

Peter opened his mouth to speak, but nothing came out. The tall man pushed himself away from the wall and came over, arm outstretched.

"How rude of me, you must forgive my manners. My name is Samuel, Samuel Tan."

He seemed taller than Peter had first thought. He had to be one hundred and ninety centimetres at least, lean, almost ascetic looking, but still there was strength in his grip as he bent over to grasp Peter's hand. Now, he scrutinised Peter with a long mournful face. His intense brown eyes were flecked with yellow, like a dog Peter had once owned.

"No real damage," Samuel said. "I think you'll find your tongue has stopped bleeding now. Good." He stepped back and flashed a shy smile, waving towards the window. "I've put everything on hold out there for a bit until we've had time to talk. We don't, however, have that much time, so I'd appreciate it if you could try and keep up.

"You, Peter Fallow, are a writer, or were until you forgot how. Instead of just continuing to float happily on the Sea of Creativity, you threw out an anchor and thought everything would stay as it was. By the time you realised the tide had gone out, leaving you stranded, it was too late. But I can fix all that. I am a muse. I can be *your* muse, Peter, but in return you need to do something for me. We need to come to an Agreement. Oh, here, I'll just show you, it'll save time. Hold my hand."

Peter saw his hand rise up and grip Samuel's. He felt a jolt. He jerked forward; a warm pleasant feeling was creeping up his arm, as if it was being gradually immersed in a tepid bath. When it reached his shoulder and moved into his head, he gasped. He had his book. It was all laid out, scene by perfect scene.

Samuel removed his hand and Peter felt, rather than saw, the images begin to fade. "No. No," he cried.

"Oh, don't worry, I can bring it back. I just need you to concentrate on other things now."

Peter frowned. One part of his head was racing down brain-alleys after the vanishing book, whilst another was blinking, "TILT, TILT, TILT" in red lights. Samuel was speaking again.

"I'm in the, er, trading business. I trade things: ideas, inspiration, success, whatever people want really, in return for an Agreement."

"What sort of agreement?"

"That's not important right now, Peter, but what I want from you is. You see, all this trading creates a lot of administration and that's really not my strong suit. I'm a dealer. I need someone to keep it all together for me. In short, I need you, Peter."

"Me? But I'm a writer, not a . . . bookkeeper."

"Ah, but, you see, I need someone far more layered than a simple bookkeeper. I need someone that can keep everything in their head, not in a ledger: characters, relationships, families, deals, and all the associated subterfuge. Just like one of your books, really. I loved *The Algernon Chronicles,* by the way; complex, disparate at times, but incredible how you brought it all together in the end. How you can just walk around with lives and secrets and sub-plots stacked in your head amazes me. No, you're ideal for the job, believe me."

Peter stared blankly. He wanted desperately to get up, but was afraid that if he did he would find himself back in his car careering towards oncoming traffic. He shook the thought away.

"And for this you give me my book? The book that I . . . saw."

"And the next, and the next, as many as you want."

"Who are you?"

Samuel sighed and reached two fingers into his vest pocket. "My card."

The name, Samuel A. Tan, seemed to stand out in huge red letters.

Peter shook his head in confusion. Samuel raised his eyes to the ceiling.

"First two initials plus the surname makes . . . ."

"What?" Peter felt himself chuckling, then laughing. He laughed so hard that tears streamed down his cheeks and he doubled over.

Samuel folded his arms and waited.

Peter pointed at Samuel. "You're . . . you're . . . Satan?" he managed to say, then burst out laughing again.

"Well, not exactly. It's more of a branding thing. BB prefers it that way. He says it drives the brand more if we all operate under the same trade mark license. I've got to tell you, it's never been the same since we corporatised. Now we have targets for everything. And more administration."

"They've corporatised hell?" Peter started laughing again. "Oh . . . I don't know why I'm laughing. If this wasn't so weird, it would be freaky. Who is BB, or shouldn't I ask? . . . .Oh, no, don't tell me," and he was off again.

"Yes, he's the big cheese, Beelzebub. He likes us to call him BB. Team building he calls it." Samuel waited politely until Peter's laughter died down.

"So, Peter, do we have an Agreement?"

"We haven't looked at the alternative. What happens if I say no."

Samuel sighed again and waved his hand. A startling image of a car sliding in slow motion towards a semi-trailer filled Peter's head.

"Not much of choice."

"On the contrary. That's what so few of you realise. There is always choice. Free will; it's your divine gift. That's what makes you all so valuable to BB. You are all gods-in-training."

Peter thought furiously. He couldn't believe he was actually buying into this, but the memory of that perfect plot, those wonderful characters burned like an afterimage in his brain. He wanted that book and, if it meant horsetrading with this whacko, then . . . "Bring it on," he said.

Samuel smiled and they shook hands. Peter felt something shift within him, like his point of balance readjusting and resettling; nothing more.

"Miles Bryce. He is cheating on his wife and his mistress. We are working with his wife so that mistress number one walks in on Miles while he is doing number two. M1 ends up shooting him in a jealous rage so our client gets the inheritance."

Peter nodded, scribbling into a small notebook. It was the third notebook in three days. Talk about story ideas; whoever or whatever Samuel A. Tan thought he might be, Peter had enough ideas to fill two volumes for the rest of his natural life. Plus, Barbara was over the moon with the first three chapters he'd already sent her. Three chapters in three days—who'da thunk . . . .

"Peter, pay attention. We're coming up for the fourth quarter review and I'm still six per cent down on my soul power target for the year. I can't afford to drop back to demon second grade. If my grading goes, so does my power, and so do your books. Hell, you have no idea just how hard it is dealing with the lowlife second-grade market. There, it's all about volume, no relationships. Just sell, sell, sell."

"You make it all sound so clinical."

"No, Peter, it's business. Now, listen up, this is where it gets complicated. Unbeknown to the wife, we have also taken a subsequent larger Agreement out with Mistress number one who actually loves this creep. So, instead of Miles getting shot, I will arrange for the wife to walk in on the lot of them and shoot the other mistress by mistake. She gets a 'go straight to jail card' and doesn't collect the inheritance. Mistress number one gets to keep Miles. In a couple of months, I'll convince the mistress that she can trade off a few more friends and family to get the wife out of the way—that's easy in jail—and then she can marry Miles the creep and the whole thing starts all over again. That's what we call a reverberator. Double credits for those you know."

"So why was the mistress's Agreement more valuable than the wife's?"

"Oh, the mistress upped the ante, of course. She put up the lives of three of her close friends and a half brother. The half brother doesn't mean much, but I took him anyway because the irony of the whole thing tickled me."

"How can she put up the lives of her friends?"

"I told you: gods-in-training. Every time you walk down the street, you are choosing, albeit subconsciously, not to kill, rape, or plunder everybody that passes. Yet you could, if you choose, do just that. I'm just adding some middleman value to the supply chain. They still pull the virtual trigger. I just supply the gun and make sure it's properly aimed. The Karma is still the same. Now, how's the book coming along?"

A week later, Peter's head was bulging with relationship networks. It was like playing chess with ten people at once, and having to think four moves ahead for each. Samuel was into meltdown mode, firing out

Agreements, then overriding them with one, sometimes two others. Peter kept it all on track, pointing out several overlapping or conflicting Agreements that would end with a neutral outcome. Samuel was deliriously grateful, as with year-end figures due, he was only just meeting his targets. Any that ended neutrally would leave him short and BB wasn't into excuses or "if onlys"; he was purely results driven and pretty ugly when he didn't get them. In a perverse sort of way, Peter was starting to enjoy it all. He was already onto the next novel. Of course, he'd had to agree to sacrifice Barbara, Janet and an ex-wife (who Samuel said hardly counted because there needed to be an emotional attachment). Besides, with a blockbuster novel being fast tracked for a Christmas release, Peter probably would need a better agent anyway.

Samuel burst into the shop, throwing his hands into the air. "Oh, thank BB and his host that that's all over for another year. I made it with one Agreement to spare. I get my promotion. Pay homage to the newest FA, grade 1."

"FA?"

"Fallen Angel. I get my wings next week, then it's goodbye Brisbane, hello overseas posting. From then on, I'll be working exclusively with just one or two major clients: military and political types mostly. They're into big numbers those guys, believe me. You should see my target for the first quarter."

"You're leaving?" Peter felt his mouth go dry. He still wasn't sure whether he could actually write anything on his own any more. "So does that mean our Agreement is concluded? Or will I go with you?"

"Concluded? With me?" Samuel laughed. "You still don't get it, do you? Poor boy."

"Get what?"

"You've been stitched up. You've already got more Karmic debt than any soul can carry. You need to find someone to take it on for you, like I did with you—of course, you will have to work your way up to where I was."

"What do you mean?" Peter felt strangely light-headed.

"Bottom of the ladder. Don't worry, you'll have plenty of time; I've managed to negotiate immortality for you—bit of a bonus. Of course, it'll take some getting used to at first. It's not easy where you're going, but I felt I owed you one—finding a suitable karmic mule brings in triple credits. I wouldn't have made it except for you."

"Going? Where . . . what . . . " Peter reached out his hand towards Samuel. He could see right through it. "My arm," he said, looking down, "my body. I'm transparent."

"Translucent actually. You won't go fully transparent for a day or so yet. But you'll be amazed at how easy it is to be a little impish voice inside people's heads, tempting, tempting and finally zing, you get one. Bit like fishing. Do you like fishing, Peter?"

"But . . . . .what about all my books? You said . . . "

"Oh, Peter, do grow up. You can still write. Haven't you ever heard of ghost writers?"

FACT: THE DEVIL IS IN THE DETAIL

Hugh C. Gray

It was 11 p.m. and I had just settled down in my armchair with a nice cup of coffee when the phone on the table beside me started to ring. I let it ring three times before I picked it up and said, "Hello, Mason Grant here. Can I help you?"

A voice I recognized as that of my American publisher said, "Mason, hi! It's John Spitz here. Just a quick call. We've finished going over your latest manuscript with our legal people. I told them you always check everything thoroughly, yet still they're worried there could be some possibility of slander et cetera. Mason, my friend, I am happy to go with your judgment. All I need from you right now is for you to tell me that you have checked your facts and all your sources, *and* you've got signed statements on file."

I pondered the question for just a few seconds and replied, "John, I have been selling books to your company now for nearly twenty years and you should know I always check my facts and double check my sources. It's something I'm most fastidious about. So you can tell your legal people there is not a problem. Everything in the manuscript is one hundred per cent checked and double-checked and, yes, I have signed statements from all my sources."

"Okay, Mason, I thought that would be the way it was, but you know them legal guys. Hell, we pay them enough, but it seems I'm the one who's got to keep *them* happy. You stay healthy, my friend. We'll talk again before the book launch. Bye for now," and with that he hung up.

Poor John, I thought, he's a multi millionaire and still works twenty hours a day—never a day off, never any time for small talk. Such a busy man! No way to lead a life.

I got up from my chair, walked across the room to a large filing cabinet, bent down and pulled open the bottom drawer. Inside was a large bottle of single malt whisky. Its seal was unbroken and next to it was a crystal glass wrapped in a plastic dust jacket. The label on the bottle said the whisky was twelve years old when it had been bottled, and I hadn't touched a drop of it in twenty years. I guess I'd never found the right occasion to open it. But the call from my publisher had started me thinking. Yes, I do always check my facts. It's important to verify the identity of the person you are talking to, to make sure their sources of information are valid.

I removed the dust cover from the glass and poured myself a hearty measure or, as John Spitz would say, a good four fingers. I took the bottle and glass back to the armchair and slowly sipped the first whisky that had passed my lips in a long long time.

I gazed across to my desk where my computer was still switched on, the monitor displaying the blank page of my next chapter. It was just begging me to type a few words. The computer was the latest model, not like the slow old P4 I used to have, but there were times when it didn't matter how fast or how slow your computer was: nothing would come out, because there was nothing going in—a common problem with writers old and new. You sit at the keyboard, or with a blank pad in your hand, and wait, willing your brain to spill out some magic story, a script, a novel, or even just a few words to break the drought. But nothing comes. Writer's block, they call it. I call it Constipated Mind Syndrome or CMS for short.

My thoughts drifted back twenty years, to a little office I had set up in the back of my Brisbane flat as a young writer. I used to spend night after night sitting at my computer, working between midnight and 5 a.m. I remembered one night just sitting there, with a blank page before me, suffering the dreaded CMS. After three hours of staring at it, I leaned back in my chair, with my arms at full stretch and shouted at the top of my voice. "God, why can't I write something?"

I surprised myself that I had shouted out loud in my frustration, but then I shrugged my shoulders and said to myself, "So what, there's nobody to hear me; even God's not listening. He's probably in bed like everyone else who is remotely sane."

I had a long stretch and a yawn. I was just about to switch off the computer and head to bed when I heard that little "ding" that told me I had incoming email. Well, I thought, I may as well check who could be contacting me at this ungodly hour in the morning, perhaps a writer colleague also suffering from CMS. I opened the mail program and clicked on the new message. It read:

I was listening. I did hear you.

I looked around the room, even though I was sure nobody was there. I double-checked to make sure my microphone wasn't plugged into my PC. Was somebody playing a joke on me? *Who is this?* I typed, but before I could send the message, new words appeared rapidly beneath it:

It's me, God. You said I wasn't listening. I was busy with a new intake, but now I'm having a break. So what's your problem?

I thought I was going mad but, hell, I'm a writer; it goes with the turf. *Okay*, I typed, *maybe I'll play along with you.*

Please yourself. You can deny me if you wish, but that does not mean I don't exist. Anyway, Mason, I am here now and I will listen to all your gripes. I'm having a break from the gate, so let's make it interesting.

Well, we started chatting about my writing and how I couldn't think of anything to write about. He gave me some advice, said that I would get my opportunities. He told me some things that surprised me, not what I would have expected to hear from God, but I had never really spoken to him before. We talked for hours, had a good old yarn, and before I knew it I had lost all sense of time. If this guy on the other end of the internet was God or not it didn't really matter. I was getting on with him really well. He sounded like a nice bloke. And spooky as it may seem, he really seemed to know what I was thinking and what I needed to know. I looked up from my monitor for a moment and realised the sun was shining in my office window and reflecting over my desk. I glanced at the clock on the wall. It was 5.50 a.m. I had been chatting to this guy or God for over three hours. On the monitor, the following words appeared:

Well, it looks like I have a queue forming at the gate. Must have been a busy night—lots of drunk drivers getting themselves killed and they end up at my gate. I have another intake to process, so I had better go and do my duties. It has been nice talking to you, but before I go do you have any questions you want to ask me?

Sheepishly, I typed: *Yes. Will I ever be a good writer?*

He replied: *Good writer? You are already a great writer. In fact, when you die, I have you pencilled in to become one of my staff writers. One more question before I go.*

Can you tell me, are there any of my family in Heaven?

And he replied: *Yes, I am sure there are, but I too have some down here with me.*

I was stunned. *What do you mean down here? I thought you said you were God?*

I am. But didn't you notice that my email address is god@underworld.org? Some people refer to me as the Devil or Lucifer, but really I am God of the Underworld. I prefer God for short. Sometimes people mix me up with the god upstairs. They should check their facts.

And next time, Mason, don't be so impatient. Think about it: there are millions of people who call me every day. It's just like your emails; I have to sort out the good from the bad. Anyway, Mason, nice talking to you. I must go. See you when you get here. Bye . . .

With that he was gone.

Since that day I have always double-checked my facts, every detail. I like to know exactly who I am talking to.

They say the Devil is in the detail. If they only knew my story.

Oh, and just so everyone knows how I feel, I don't want to be a staff writer . . . I'm not sure that I want to go to hell either, but I'm still working that angle out.

I finished the whisky, and placed the glass on the table at the side of my armchair. Just then, I glanced across the room at my computer. A yellow circle appeared on the screen, followed by eyes, a mouth, et cetera. It was an old Smiley icon.

I thought to myself, That's odd: I had never seen a picture drawn before my eyes before. I walked across the room for closer look and noticed the Smiley had horns. It may be the drink, but I still think: The Devil is in the detail.

DEVIL'S DEBRIEF

Lea Greenaway

There is no rest for the wicked in my line of work. I like it that way. That continuous chorus of "Oh, go to the devil!", "Devil take you!", "The devil you will!" is music to my ears—affirmation, you know; it confirms my continued presence in the marketplace.

I welcome the onslaught, but if there is one group I could cheerfully say "Go to hell" to, no pun intended, it's those writers. Bane of my existence, they are: such a carping, whinging, self-obsessed lot. Comes of being such a solitary occupation, I suppose. They never get those anti-social corners knocked off by the rough and tumble of normal social intercourse.

I can see you don't believe me. Let me give you an example.

Just the other day this woman was carrying on—fiftyish she was. She had decided writing would provide meaning in her miserable life now she had given up real work. There she was, sitting at her computer whining, "I'd sell my eye teeth to the devil to become a successful author."

Now firstly, I don't do eye teeth—not at all marketable and, secondly, she thinks I'm going to pay something? Puh-leeze!

I blame Marlowe. Ever since he wrote *Faust* all these arty types have

106

been trying one on. I confess that by dint of some very long spoons some of them have managed to pull it off.

Unfortunately, part of the job description imposed by management—no negotiation there; outmoded labour practices, et cetera—is I have to respond to every direct offer.

"You rang, madam?" I said in my best *Remains of the Day* voice. I rather like the opportunities the job gives me for character acting.

She jumped, swinging round in her chair.

"You rang?" I repeated in her other ear.

"Who said that?" She looked wildly around the pokey little room and even under the desk.

"I understand an offer of eye teeth was made, madam. I regret to say there is no current demand for eye teeth. However, you did call upon me. Is there something you require?"

"What?" She had the look of a woman who has decided she's finally lost it.

"I believe your actual words were: 'I'd sell my eye teeth to the devil to become a successful author.'"

"The devil!" She gasped. "Oh, my God, I've called up the devil."

I winced. "Yes, madam," I prompted.

I wish I hadn't. Out came this petty diatribe about her precious novel: was it young adult, or speculative adult fiction? Was there a strong enough plot to sustain a short novel, or would it be better as a short story? Were there too many characters?

Honestly, they seem to think I care. As I said, it is a very solitary occupation. When they get the chance these authors prattle endlessly about their pathetic bits of work. You should have heard how Tolstoy carried on. He gave me no end of trouble, and the number of drafts I had to edit for him. I almost gave up the whole idea of war I got so bored with it; I decided peace was easier.

I tuned back in.

" . . . so if you could just go through it and give me your opinion and perhaps have a word with a suitable publisher when you have decided what genre it is." She looked pleadingly, in quite the wrong direction as it happened; I was behind her again.

"There is," I reminded her, "the small matter of payment. Unfortun . . . ."

"Oh," she interrupted, "yes, I guess I could get my dentist to take them out and could have them for you by," she glanced down at her calendar, "the end of next week?"

"Madame," I said testily, "I don't take eye teeth."

Her face fell.

"I will assist you, however, on the condition that you agree to everlasting torment in the next life."

"Torment? Torment! What do you think I have been suffering for the past year?" she shrieked. All the frustration, self doubt and general angst surfaced. "I don't want your everlasting torment, what do you think writing does to me now? If you won't take my eye teeth and make me an overnight success, you can just piss off!"

That's another part of the job description. If they dismiss you, you have to go. So I obliged and left an acrid puddle on her carpet. As I left, I heard her voice receding into the distance, "I'll bloody well take up poetry, so there!"

Modern manners! Where's the commitment? At least Tolstoy had staying power. Bah, you can keep these writers—whingers, the lot of them.

DOONICE

Kris Hembury

Orange afternoon was darkening. Madison leaned on the sandstone wall that lined the Brisbane River, scribbling down notes for the novel he longed to begin. The clear breeze pressed on his face and fondled the pages of his notepad. He smiled and waved at a friendly bunch of passengers aboard the City Cat that whirred past.

To his astonishment, a penguin sprung out of the waters. Its bulging belly cushioned its landing on the wall, and it dragged behind it a sloppy manuscript that it thumped down in front of him.

"What . . . the . . . " said Madison.

"Twelve-hundred pages of perfect prose—if I do say so myself!"

After his gawking session, Madison looked down at the gluggy mess: twelve-hundred pages! That would need some editing, he thought as he scrunched his face and peeled back a few pages.

"Very . . . wet. And long."

The penguin opened its beak and blasted out hot dry air, like a bathroom hand-drier on steroids. The pages flapped completely dry, and Madison's hair blew into a devilishly good-looking style, which he could see reflected in a mirror the penguin had pulled out from under its wing.

"The new you," said the penguin. "Much hotter."

"Okay," Madison swallowed. 'Crazy' sufficiently described his uncle-in-law, the tree herder, but not this. "So you've written a novel? Good job."

"No, Madison. *You've* written a novel," he said.

"You know my name?"

"Yeah, like that's a surprise. Hmm . . . I know your name because it means, 'strength in battle'—the precise trait I'm after. That's why I'm talking to you and not that sexy bird over there."

Madison wasn't sure if the penguin was looking at a nearby ibis, whose beak was ready to dip into the garbage bin, or at the Scottish man shouting obscenities at the bird.

Madison hadn't realised penguin-beaks could form smiles, let alone wicked ones. The penguin then offered him the manuscript, absolutely no questions asked, on the condition that he did him one 'teeny-weeny' favour.

"Are you the devil?" asked Madison, not wanting to offend, but thinking it was best to sort out the relationship before making any decisions. Plus, there was the whole penguin suit thing.

The penguin made a quacking, chirping noise, and then a menacing laugh resounded in Madison's head. It didn't hurt. In fact, it kind of tickled, but anything going on inside his head eventually annoyed him.

"Please. It's impolite to laugh at people."

The laughing continued as if it came from elsewhere, while the penguin, still quacking, managed to squeeze out some words.

"Me, the devil! Are you are aware I'm a penguin?"

Eventually, the evil laughter and the quacking stopped.

"I am Neddy—the devil's right-hand man." He leaned close to Madison and whispered behind one flipper, "He likes a grand entrance, which is really why I'm here." Neddy held up both flippers and announced, "Introducing, the red guy himself. The one you mortal peasants know as the devil. The benevolent (sometimes deceptive) master himself: Mr Doonice!"

Neddy cheered and clapped his flippers. Madison scanned his surrounds for a giant demon, or for any evil looking entity: a snake, a seductive woman, even a man with a moustache. Nothing.

Neddy nudged his head towards a lady-beetle flying in from behind him. It veered past his head and did a loop, before touching down beside the manuscript. It ruffled its gold-speckled wings.

Neddy spoke. "Can you believe he thought I was you? I don't even have proper wings!"

The lady-beetle reared up on its hind legs.

"Silence, scab!" Its voice roared, and Madison realised this was the person . . . creature . . . thing's laugh that had bounced around his brain.

"You needn't shout, Mr . . . Devil," said Madison. A teenage boy walked past and looked at him strangely.

"I'm not shouting! This is my regular voice, and I refuse to whisper. And you will call me by my new millennium title: Mr Doonice. Why? Because I like the ring of it!"

Madison shrugged. "Make all the noise you like. If you want to draw attention . . . "

"I won't draw attention! Nobody can hear us. Neddy and I exist only in your perception. I like it this way because Neddy can be a penguin—a creature clearly not native to Brisbane, but which he really likes—and I can be amused as passers-by make strange faces because they think you're talking to yourself."

An elderly couple crept past, their faces furrowed like . . . most old people's actually.

"See." The devil ruffled its little gold wings. "Anyway, did you accept the offer?"

Neddy stepped forward. "I haven't finished describing the terms yet, Your Gluttonous Pigship."

Madison couldn't resist smiling as Mr Doonice huffed, and folded his widdle front legs.

"Fine. Hurry up then," said Doonice.

Neddy cleared his throat. "Yes, so the manuscript is 'yours'"—Madison thought watching a penguin signal quotes with his flippers was as cute as watching a lady-beetle throw practice punches, which Doonice was—"on the following condition. You must accept and fully participate in . . . " Neddy cleared his throat before continuing, "a duel with His Magnificent Scalper."

"This Devil? Mr Doonice?" asked Madison.

"The only devil, the Pummelling Pillager himself. The Sensitive-Region Interrogator, the Ball—"

"Alright Neddy, he gets it." Doonice threw his front legs in the air, then folded them. "So, Madison, are we agreed?"

Madison scratched his forehead with his pen. "Let me make sure I'm not . . . completely crazy. If I fight you . . . "

"In the form I'm currently in," Doonice clarified.

"Right, as a lady-beetle. Then I can have the manuscript?"

"Correct, scum."

"Pardon my straightforwardness, but is it any good? Your book, I mean."

Neddy stepped forward and lifted his chin. "It is the greatest work of the new millennium. Just as you have been endeavouring to write, it is a story of the struggle for happiness. The main character is known as Nedy." His eyes looked between Doonice's and Madison's. "One D."

Madison scratched the back of the pen up and down his chin.

"So you wrote it?" He pointed at Neddy.

"No." He stretched onto tiptoes and winked conspicuously, "*You* wrote it. As in—"

"He gets it!" roared Doonice as he sauntered towards Madison. "But does he agree?"

Madison looked out over the grey ripples of the river, and up at the CBD tower blocks that were starting to light up with reds and yellows as night fell. His eyes returned to Doonice.

"It doesn't make sense. Why fight? Why me? Why as a lady-beetle?"

"Because you can't stop change. I've had this 'devil' job since the lovely Eve was waltzing about. Tempting people, causing suffering; I've done all the naughty stuff, and sure I chose my path, but even devils can learn from their mistakes. I fell, but now I want to pick myself up like so many catchy songs suggest. Problem is, the big boy upstairs says it's only official if I'm defeated in a fair duel by someone mortal, and nice. Sounds weird, I know. Something to do with quantum mechanics.

"So can we fight? It's a good novel; I've read it. Definitely Neddy's best." He then whispered, as best as the burning voice of the devil can, which is not at all, "Not including his other work, *The Lord of the Rings*, or *War and Peace*." He coughed. "Or *Wuthering Heights*, not to mention the entire works of Shakespeare." He cleared his throat.

Madison stared out at the darkness and light moving on the water. It seemed like nobody would be hurt if he accepted the manuscript. Except the devil, of course, but rumour suggested he was long overdue for a hiding.

"If I win, which I presume you want since you're fighting as a lady-beetle, then what happens to the world?"

Neddy responded, almost dreamily, "Bliss. Eden. Heaven on earth. It's unimaginable. No more suffering, despair, or staying back after five."

Doonice quickly stepped in. "Ahh, yes, anyway ... ready to fight?"

Madison looked at him suspiciously.

He looked nervous, and quickly said, "You know, I'm just recalling the novel's climax. Oh my goodness! When Nedy ... did that thing ... to those. Ah crap. Okay, I didn't finish it. But not because it's bad, it's because I find those sorts of books too sad. Anyway, I guarantee it'll make you famous and publishers will want more, which is the important thing. Can we fight now?" Doonice started throwing punches.

"If the world becomes fully content, then no-one will want to read a novel about striving for happiness!"

Doonice's swinging front legs dropped and his eyes met Neddy's. "Damn. He got it." He looked back towards Madison. "So, the manuscript idea was just some motivation. Don't you want to be responsible for destroying evil anyway? Come on, let's fight." He threw a few right and left hooks.

Madison leaned on the wall and tapped his fingers. He could destroy evil, or he could take the manuscript and be what he'd always wanted to be: a writer.

Another ferry whirred by in the night. He smiled, grabbed the manuscript and ran.

Neddy and Doonice smiled at one another as they wandered along the smooth sandstone wall.

"I was getting worried there," said Doonice. "Sure, my schemes to make people act selfishly are getting more and more intricate . . . "

"Which means more fun," Neddy interjected.

"Yes, which means more fun. But I'm such a good actor—throwing those punches—I thought he might choose to fight. I think it's time I stopped taking such risks. He could have won, you know. Imagine that!"

"Oh, Your Grubbiness. You know writers—conceited bunch. They'd squeeze a small dog into a juice bottle and throw it into a campfire if it meant finding a good story. You had it in the bag from the beginning, and you know it, you cheeky devil."

Doonice sighed as if bored. "You're right. You know, I wonder when he'll realise the manuscript is just his diary repeated over and over."

Neddy chuckled. "Probably about the same time he writes his novel!"

AND THE DEEP BLUE SEA

Robert Hoge

Silently, the ferry sliced the surface of the water, dividing the river into quarters. On the left bank lay the city—office lights beginning to glow at the start of Brisbane's short twilight. On the right, the houses of the rich—double-storeyed, with tennis courts, swimming pools and pontoons. In the center was Derek Wagner—his past tumbling behind him in the gentle wake of the ferry and, before him, his future: an endless burning sunset.

Wagner stood at the bow of the ferry, his back turned to the water. He nervously stroked the denim of his of jeans as he searched the boat. At the rear was the ferry's gate. He'd used it thousands of times, getting on and off, in his daily journeys on the river. In the middle, there were thirty-nine seats—Wagner had counted them once—enclosed in a cabin that locked them away from the elements. At the front, where Wagner always travelled, was a wide-open section with a few seats and plenty of standing room. Mostly, he sat and let the air wash over his face. Even in the depths of a hot summer, the air coming off the river was always cool. He liked the clarity of its smell, and he often breathed it in so deeply that he felt energized by its freshness, felt alive and ready to write. At other times, he stood and leaned into the wind, daring it to knock him down. But this evening, he was focused on the passengers—trying to work out which one had come to take his life.

Whispers yanked him out of his paranoia.

The night was quickening. Wagner studied the dark carefully; he was sure there were only three other passengers aboard. One waited at the rear of the ferry, seemingly eager to depart. Nearby stood an elderly couple. The woman's gray hair flashed golden as it caught the city lights, but the couple's faces were hidden in darkness. The man's face seemed to darken even more as Wagner stared at it. He searched for details—his nose, a crease in his brow, his eyes—his eyes, for god's sake, his eyes—but there was only the darkness.

So he listened.

Wagner had heard such whispers before of course: "Are you *sure* it's him . . . "; "Excuse me, aren't you . . . "; "It couldn't possibly be . . . "; "Didn't he write that one . . . "; "I don't mean to impose, but could you possibly sign . . . "

He'd come to hate the whispers and the smiles, and the handshakes and the supplication that came with them. He despised all of it. The whispers, the words. The deal he'd made.

Wagner looked down, shook his head. He looked up again and saw the old man had crossed from the opposite side of the front deck.

"Excuse me. I'm sorry to bother you, but are you by any chance Derek Wagner, the author?"

Wagner smiled bitterly and slipped a quiet 'yes' in between his second and third nod.

"Well, what a lovely surprise," the old man said, then turned his head. "See dear, I told you. Come say hello."

Wagner smiled at the woman briefly and looked behind her to watch the other passenger.

"Lovely to meet you," the woman said.

"I'm Chris, and this is my wife, Kimberley. We love your work."

116

"I adored *The Pilgrim's Bridge*," Kimberley said.

"Thank you," Wagner said. He felt the ferry gently nudge the wharf as it docked at its next stop. It rocked gently on the waves. "It's a pleasure to meet people who enjoy what I do. And you know, I can't keep writing the books if you don't keep buying them."

The captain tied the ferry down and opened the gate to allow the passengers to disembark. It made a cold eerie creak in the suddenly still air. Wagner shivered. The couple blocked his view of the stern and he had to glance over the old man's shoulder to see if any new passengers where waiting to board.

"Waiting for someone?" Chris asked.

"No. Yes. Sort of. A bit preoccupied, that's all."

"Well, this is our stop. We'd best be going," Kimberley said.

"Yes, right. It was lovely meeting you, Mister Wagner." They walked to the far end of the ferry, nodding at the captain as they departed.

"Keep up the writing, Derek," Kimberley yelled as they crossed to the wharf. "At this rate your next book will be bigger than the Bible."

"Of all the books that could help," he said to himself, "that one is of least use to me."

He smiled despite himself and waved them goodbye. Searching the boat again, Wagner found he was the final passenger. A shadow fell across the deck in front of him. He looked down at his worn sandals and said, "Are you to ferry me to the gates of hell? Or am I to wade through this river that is to be my end?"

"I will take you," the captain replied, "to the gates of hell, and beyond."

The ferry captain looked nothing like Wagner imagined Satan should. And nothing at all like he had when they first met twenty-seven years ago. He was wearing the standard uniform—a crisp white button-up shirt with a city logo emblazoned on the left breast pocket, navy blue shorts and a braided captain's cap. Wagner stood looking at

117

him for a long silent moment, trying to spot some evidence of evil—a red flicker to the eyes, a slight sniff of sulfur, anything that would reassure him that it was really happening. But there was nothing. No twitch of nose or twist of tail. But he was a head taller than Wagner, and when he leant down to speak to him, the writer was forced to close his eyes for a moment to escape the intensity of his stare.

"You know one thing I can't understand?" the captain said.

Wagner shrugged, trying to hide his fear. "What?"

"Why people sit inside these things when they could be out in the breeze, and the sun, and the air."

"It's easier to live smaller lives when you're inside," Wagner said. "We live such indoor lives—most of us—small homes, smaller offices, the smallest of possible lives that don't require us to do anything big with our hearts or our heads."

"Huh," the captain shrugged, "best I'd come up with was because they maybe just didn't like the wind."

Wagner nodded and turned away to look down the river, hoping he would catch a breeze that would cool him down and lower his heart rate. The ferry rounded the city reach. Now, it was coming up on the Gateway Bridge, which shot up high into the air like a rocket ship runway out of an old space movie.

"Do you ever wonder why smart people make the deal?" Wagner asked.

"People make the deal every day, Derek. Just not with me. They trade off fast food comfort for a fat and diseased final few years. People smoke, don't exercise, drink too much. All of it for short term gain."

"Actually," Wagner said, "I don't smoke. And remind me—just which of the Ten Commandments was 'thou shall not partake of fast food'?"

The captain stepped closer and Wagner felt a warmth that made him shiver.

"Not going to try to get out of it, Derek—most people do, you know—try to strike a new bargain?"

"I'd suspect that," Wagner said. He turned back towards the captain. "But we made a deal. I got twenty-seven years of writing at the top of my game—prolific, flawless sentence structure, poetic when I wanted, driven when needed, feted by critics, adored by readers, award-winning *and* best-selling."

"And I get your eternal soul, to suffer in the pit of damnation for all of eternity," the captain said.

Wagner sucked in his breath as the ferry's engines died suddenly.

The captain smiled and, in that moment, Wagner saw a flash of the devil in his eyes.

"You know the sad reality that will stay with you, Derek? You'll never know how good you might have been without my help. You'll never know what stories you may have written, what books of wonder, what startling tales you could have told without me. Perhaps, someday, I'll let you look into that other life. Either way, I win. You find out that without me you would have been nothing—a nobody. Or you find out that you made a redundant deal and you really didn't need me after all."

The ferry drifted on the water. Wagner looked out over the river.

"Would you like to know the secret? How I made you such a great writer?"

"Sure," Wagner said.

"It's this place. This river that you love so much," the captain said.

"I don't understand."

"That's not true, Derek. You've felt it every time you've come onto this river. See, I can't simply wish you a better writer. It's not that easy. All I can do is facilitate what's already there."

Wagner laughed. "I haven't got a clue what it might be, but sure as hell the sign at the front gate to your place doesn't read: 'Satan: the great facilitator'."

The captain smiled. "I'm not a magician. I have powers, but to enact change those powers have to focus on something. For you, it was this river—this river that flows through the middle of your city."

Wagner looked at the rippled reflection of the moon upon the water and knew he was being told the truth. He had always been drawn to the river. He always felt more alive when he was on it, ready to get the next word on the page—hungry for it.

"How did you do it?" Wagner asked.

"I'm older than the river; older than the water, older than the bedrock and the silt; older than the memories it carries—the lies, the hopes, the despair. Older than the stories. Older than your stories, Derek. So old that I have many tricks. And one of them is that for you, and only you, Derek, this river is a conduit. It collects those memories, the hopes, the love and despair, the myths and the truths of the people in this city and funnels them into you. You already had such a love of this river. It was the easiest way."

"Yes, I do love the river," Wagner admitted.

"You know, one other thing I never managed to understand, Derek? Why, if you loved being out here on this river so much, you never learned to swim?"

Too late, Wagner felt a sharp force in the middle of his back. He tumbled over the side of the ferry and into the river. As he went under, he whacked his head against the hull and swallowed a lungful of water.

It was there before he heard it really. The sound of a scream yet to start—gurgling above him. The river's waves seemed to swallow him, as he tried desperately to reach the surface. Then he heard a voice, and felt himself rising up through the water and the mud it carried. It was the captain's voice, or at least part of it was.

"You made a deal twenty-seven years ago and I'm here to collect. Derek Wagner, do you come willingly, as you agreed to in blood half a lifetime ago?"

Wagner's lungs were screaming at him to breathe. He broke through the surface, spat out a mouthful of water and wished he hadn't sent the elderly couple—the last of his readers he'd ever encounter—away so quickly.

The water claimed him again, sucking him down. It was getting colder and heavier as it soaked into his jeans. Above him, Wagner saw a flaming red figure lean over the side of the ferry and, beneath the figure, a short length of rope hanging down from one of the ferry's anchor points. He grabbed for it, but the rope slipped through his wet hands, and he slipped beneath the surface for a third time.

Wagner had chosen to deal with the devil and should have guessed that the climax of his story would be just as painful as its postscript. His chest was burning—it felt like the same hunger he had to write; burning him up from the inside, making a fiery pit inside his chest that needed to work its way out. He was burning hot and warming the water around him. He needed the words, needed the air. The end of the rope was glowing red and swinging above him. He felt the water rising around him. But he was still so hungry, still had so much to say. Wagner stretched his arm and grabbed for the rope again. He felt his fingers close around it. Quickly, he wrapped it around his wrist and pulled himself above the surface.

"Wait," Wagner yelled, feeling the burning in his chest. "I've got a proposition." He gasped for more air. "Something you might be interested in. A new deal. To write . . . "

"I've more than enough writers on the books, Derek."

"But none like me. The couple who just got off the boat. We were talking about how writers and readers needed each other. How they couldn't exist without one another." Wagner stopped and sucked in a lungful of air.

"See," he continued, "I know I didn't need the deal. You asked me before about the torment of not knowing whether I actually needed you or not. But I do know. I know what I'm capable of. I want to write one more book. A new book."

"Everyone wants one more, Derek. One more day, one more cigarette, one more chance. Your currency is books. But you're out of print, I'm afraid."

"Not my book; yours. A bible."

The hair poking out from beneath the captain's cap briefly flared red. The rope Wagner was holding started to unravel.

"Wait. No. Not *the* Bible. That's been done already. *Yours.* Someone needs to write your story. I can do that. Tell the world who you are and where you came from. In your own words."

The captain nodded and smiled to reveal bright, white teeth. "Every reader needs a writer, you say." The captain stopped for a moment and looked along the river. It was wide and stretched long before emptying into the bay. "Okay, Derek. Well played. Appeal to my natural ego and your natural talent. Very smart indeed. But—and don't you always love the but—you'll do it on your own without the help of the gift I gave you. That deal is over."

Derek smiled and felt the river washing over him in waves of relief.

"And, Derek. It better be good because there aren't going to be any sequels to this book. At least, not for you."

THE CONFÉRENCIER

Vanda Ivanovic

I am leaning against the bedstead, knees pulled up under my chin and arms wrapped tightly around my shins. My chin pivots on my knee as I look from the blank wall to the bookshelf that leans against the door leading to the hallway.

I wait. Moonlight reflects off the computer monitor on the desk.

When the music first sounds, I try to nod to myself. My chin is now firmly wedged on my knee and the movement produces a sharp pain in my neck. I whimper and stay still. Nondescript brass instruments drag out the melody, repeating the four bars over and over. I wait for the footsteps. The fading reflection in the monitor shows me the moon is setting. I stare at the edge of the desk.

The light in the room changes and I can hear the rustling of cloth. Instead of trying to nod again, I blink slowly. By now the wall has been replaced by a set of moth-eaten curtains. A semicircle of amber lights outlines the stage that extends from beneath them.

Footsteps approach. The bookshelf against the door rattles as someone in the hallway knocks on the door.

I do not move. The knocking stops and the footsteps retreat.

The music is dying down, replaced by a crisp clicking noise of tap-dancing shoes walking towards the stage. The curtains waver and move aside. A pair of puckered, maroon-painted lips stretches into a happy grin. The devil's beady black eyes shine with the glow of stage lights. His left hand smoothes the hair already plastered tightly against his scalp. In his right hand, he twirls a walking cane with a cheap nickel-plated head. When he grins at me again, I hear a sweeping metallic drum roll.

"And how is my favourite author?" the Devil asks. I stare at him blankly.

The Devil swivels on the tip of his shoe, the cracks in the lacquered leathers clearly visible in the light from the stage. He touches the top of the bookshelf daintily and his finger comes away covered in dust.

"Lovely, darling. How long has it been there this time? A day? Three days?"

"A week."

I am staring at the chipped inlays on his jacket buttons.

"Very good, darling. Anything else?" Fingers with fine nails pry a book out of the shelf. Small flakes of green nail polish fall to the ground as he turns the book over.

"I see that the first novel has been published in paperback," he says.

"Yes. The title in gold lettering and gold stickers on the front. I can see it being read in the airport lounges and being forgotten on the seats for the cleaner to pick up. Although that will probably happen with the next edition, the one that will feature the 'Now A Major Motion Picture' sticker."

"But that's just gorgeous, darling," says the Devil and grins. He deposits the paperback on the shelf and pirouettes again, this time pulling a hard-cover book from the neighbouring shelf.

"Oh, darling, why didn't you say something? A review in *Guardian Weekly*?"

"In the side column, wedged between two other nondescript novels. One more weak attempt at infusing city life with magical realism."

The Devil makes a tut-tut sound. "But that's not what the review said, darling."

I stare even harder at the row of bookshelves opposite the bed.

"That's what it will amount to," I say, moving my lips and tongue with difficulty.

The nickel tip of his cane taps out a complicated rhythm on the side of the desk.

"And this? Three separate piles of paper?" He turns to grin at me. A dull gold tooth glints for a moment.

"Short stories. I'm keeping them separate."

The Devil picks up one sheaf of paper.

"How lovely, darling. This one starts in Nazareth at the time of Saint Paul. Have you been reading Vidal's *Live from Golgotha* again?"

I try to nod again and the vertebrae in my neck click painfully, making me whimper.

"Yes, thank gods for postmodernism. It made plagiarism a valid art form. Very beneficial for those like me who cannot think of an original story even if our lives depend on it," I say.

My tear ducts overflow and now I am sniffling into my denim-covered knees.

"Oh, honey, not tears, please." A silk handkerchief, threadbare in places, presses against my left eye. Threads of disintegrating embroidery catch in my eyelashes. The bed sheet rips as I dig my booted feet further in.

"So, can we talk about the deal again, darling?"

"We did not have a deal," I reply, mispronouncing words between sobs.

The Devil shrugs expansively. Rusted bells jangle from his sleeve cuffs.

"Well, it's never too late, darling. But you already know the range of offers. Same old same old."

I swing my head slowly from side to side. The folds of the bedding are melting together in my watery vision.

"I am not interested."

"Personally, darling, I am not terrifically fond of those anymore, myself. They are all of, you know, hire purchase variety."

I am moaning quietly now. As I grit my teeth, I feel the filling in one of the molars crunch. Bits of dental cement roll around my mouth. I wail.

"And with those ones, darling, I have to wait until you are dead. Considering the terrific modern medicine and all those gorgeous mental health schemes, I would have to wait a really long time."

The Devil tugs on the lapels of his dinner jacket to straighten them. Shrivelled carnation petals float to the floor.

"So, you know, darling, who knows when and even if I would see you in that really big rocking Hell downstairs."

I roll my tongue over my teeth. Sharp pieces of filling, coated in spit, dribble down my chin.

The lights around the stage glow more brightly. The repetitive tune picks up again.

"Anyway, darling, I am getting quite used to these little, live-in, personal ones. They're really chic, especially when you artists design them."

He walks away towards the stage, turning to give me one last grin as he steps between the curtains. I open my mouth slightly, feeling the tooth marks in my lower lip.

Now that the stage has disappeared, the sunlight draws a crisp outline of the computer on the blank wall.

I stumble off the bed and push the bookshelf back into its proper place and unlock the door. My head drooping, I switch on the computer. With my head slumped into my left palm and the fingers of the right hand pecking slowly at the keyboard, I begin to write.

Yet again.

THE THIRD STAIR FROM THE TOP

Vanda Ivanovic

The Devil came to visit completely unannounced, which annoyed me, as I had not had the time to tidy up the room or wash the dirty dishes in the kitchenette. I wondered how he managed to avoid the third stair from the top. Although he politely noted that my bedsit was very cosy, I was embarrassed, which annoyed me even further.

Having removed the pile of books from the rickety armchair, he settled down nonchalantly and stretched his legs.

"You could have phoned," I said.

"The Devil is sitting in your living room—" he began.

"My only room," I interrupted.

"—and you are worrying about the state of your kitchen. Quite petty."

I sat down at the computer and lifted one pile of paper after another until I located the ashtray. Scraps of newspapers and slim volumes of literary criticism cascaded onto the floor. The keyboard beeped in protest as the second volume of the Oxford English Dictionary landed heavily on the keys. The Devil shook his head in mock sympathy.

"What a mess," he cooed.

"Take your sunglasses off," I said, exhaling smoke. He obediently removed the expensive sunglasses, revealing a pair of fox-like, gorgeous green eyes.

"Your eyelashes are too feminine," I commented. "As are the eyebrows. They ruin the impression of threatening, yet alluring sex appeal."

I am not sure if he winced or not, but I must have made him uncomfortable. Instead of responding, he fiddled with an engraved silver cigarette case, finally opening it and selecting a long, dark cigarillo. I leaned over and offered him the lighter.

"All wrong," I cautioned. "Slim cigars and mother-of-pearl inlays. What's that supposed to be, art deco?" I waved towards the cigarette case. The Devil hastily put it away. "Very weak."

He finally managed to light the cigarillo and let out a twirling plume of smoke towards me. The smoke blurred his features, but the eyes still glowed clearly.

"That is a pathetic cinematic effect, the blurred frame with a single focused point. Even Hollywood stopped using it in the late fifties."

The cigarillo fell out of his hand. I leaned over to place it in the ashtray. The Devil's exquisitely shaped fingers wrapped around my wrist.

"My dear, we need to talk," he said huskily and allowed himself a small smile, revealing a gleaming pointed incisor against the full pink flesh of his lower lip. I rolled my eyes.

"No, please. Please not vampires. It took me two years to move away from the concept of the vampire as a metaphor for repressed sexuality."

The Devil let go of my arm and flicked his hand over the cigar on the carpet, extinguishing the small flame.

"I am hear to discuss the matter of your soul," he said testily.

A small piece of paper was poking out from underneath the keyboard. I sighed.

"I see that the matter causes you some concern, as it should," the Devil said pleasantly.

I shook my head sadly. "Would you believe that I spent the whole morning looking for this?" I held up the scrap of paper with a number scribbled on it. Now I could finally call the landlord about that blasted third stair from the top.

"You have something to offer me for my soul?" I asked over my shoulder, shooing the cat away from the desktop. I sneezed as I picked black fur out of the keyboard.

"Bless you," the Devil said.

"That's an improvement," I noted. "However, a soul which can be won and lost is such an outdated Western Christian concept. You should keep more abreast of the current modes of thinking and realize the potential inherent in the dynamics of a global culture, rather than a single hegemonic discourse."

"You seek to best me in a contest of wits," he purred. "You hope to acquire the prize without paying the price."

"What prize?"

"Why, what every practitioner of your art aspires to: fortune and glory within your lifetime, fame eternal after your death, though the maws of Hell itself await you at the journey's end."

I put out my cigarette, frowning.

"Please do not use that tone of voice with me."

"What tone?" he snapped.

"The voice of the generic evil yet wise character from any work of derivative epic fantasy."

The springs in the armchairs started snapping one by one. The Devil swatted away at the cat, which had come to investigate the strange sounds.

"This attitude of yours is not going to help you."

I shrugged as I walked past him and into the kitchenette.

"You want a cup of coffee?"

The lapels of his jacket were starting to curl with heat and I could see small horns throbbing red under his forehead, trying to break out.

"Can you please do that in the bathroom?" I called over my shoulder as I searched for two clean cups. "You've already left a cigarette burn in the carpet."

"I don't have to put up with this," the Devil said and stormed out, slamming the door behind him.

I counted the thuds on the staircase. One, two, three and almost four. Then came the crash as the badly secured plank slipped off its rusted rail and broke under the infernal footsteps.

I shrugged once more, this time apologetically and opened the door. The cat peered down from between my legs. I shook my head at the hole in the staircase. Yellow steam was rising from the crumpled black suit on the ground. It carried a whiff of sulphur. The cat sneezed and I sighed again.

I don't have a writer's block, or a desire for immortality. But I really need to call the landlord about that staircase.

NEIGHBOURS

Trent Jamieson

Brisbane is a fun place to visit, but always stay on your guard. Due to its pleasant climate and rather nice outlook, the Devil is a frequent visitor. The following miscellany may prove helpful during your time here.

—From: *You and the Devil: It can be fun*

(Brisbane City Council)

I had been not long at writing, but long enough to know it wasn't going well, when the Devil, of all people, moved in next door.

"Isn't that the Devil?' my wife asked, as we came down the drive. "Well, that's a coincidence, and convenient."

I just grumbled at her.

He was directing removalists and rubbing his peaked beard. He fixed us with a stare and waved us over.

I was in no mood for talking, but my wife had other ideas.

"Welcome to the neighbourhood," she said.

The Devil grinned. "Thank you," he said.

We introduced ourselves, he shook our hands. His grip was firm, his palm slightly clammy.

"Nice to meet you," he said, "but I better get back to it; you have to watch these removalists like a hawk."

"Well, fancy that," my wife said as we unpacked our shopping. "Can you believe it?"

"I can believe it," I muttered and left her to the unpacking. I was in a bad mood; this writing thing wasn't as easy as I'd thought. The little room I'd set up as my office seemed to mock me—when I could bear to sit in it.

Fact 8: The Devil is inordinately fond of sentences that begin with, or contain, the words 'The Devil'.

"Oh, how much writing did you get done today?" my wife asked.

"Well, I did three loads of washing and I cleaned the gutters, " I grumbled and she smiled.

Fact 23: The Devil is allergic to peanuts.

One night, not long after the Devil moved in, I woke up to find him over my bedhead, my manuscript in his hands. I sat straight up. He was the last person I wanted to see it, because I knew he wouldn't like it. He smiled at me and put a finger to his lips.

"You wouldn't want to wake up your wife."

"What the hell are you doing?"

"I was looking for something to read, found your manuscript. This whole Devil storyline isn't really working now, is it? In fact, it isn't a story at all—I mean, it's a list."

Before I could defend myself and suggest that perhaps a list can work as a story, he cleared his throat and read from the manuscript. Quiet, so as not to wake my wife.

" Little Known Facts Regarding the Devil.

"Fact 1. At night, while you are asleep, the Devil will often crouch

132

over your bed, staring down, smiling; sometimes whispering; sometimes reading your favourite book and dog-earing the pages. Do not be alarmed; this is just his way of saying hello."

He chuckled. "Well you got that right. Hi there." He waved down at me. "Fact 2. The Devil likes to hang out in Toowong because that part of Brisbane is closer to Hell than anywhere else in Australia and the Devil, in his dotage, has gotten lazy. He sits there drinking coffee; not long blacks as most would think, but lattes with plenty of sugar. If he gets up and leaves his seat, do not take it; the Devil has a weak bladder and has most probably just nipped off to the toilet. He doesn't like seat stealers."

The Devil glared at me and flicked a page ahead. "Fact 5. The Devil's lungs are like sandpaper. His skin is smooth, expressions move across his face like a blemish. He's at once pretty, and hateful to look upon, and good with the ladies. Apparently, he's not much of a kisser, but he's persistent and charming . . .

"Fact 18. The Devil is fond of noise, but is very good with silence. He likes ostentation, but is a master of that space in the corner of the eye, the moment before the moment one blinks and a sliver of the moment after. A sly wink in acknowledgement of his skill, if such a moment should occur, is all that is required."

He shook his head, a little dust from his skin dropped on my pillow. "What rubbish, except facts one and four, of course, but those are obvious. Trent, this sort of stuff just doesn't work. No-one wants to read about the Devil any more, at least not in a humorous subtext. And it puts me in a bad light."

"Maybe you're right," I said.

"No maybe about it, kiddo. By the way, where did you get this information?"

I shrugged. "There's plenty of good stuff in the library."

"Library, eh. Well, you can do better than that. I'll get back to you, give you a little advice, and maybe make an offer you can't refuse. But not tonight; it's getting late."

He crawled up the ceiling, then down and out the bedroom window. I shut it firmly behind him, swearing that I would get bars installed the next day. If not to keep the Devil out, then to give me another distraction from writing.

My wife opened one eye. "I told you stories as lists don't work. You need some kind of framing device."

"You're asleep," I said.

Everyone's a critic.

Fact 10: The Devil is in the details. The more detailed the details, the more Devil. Which is why planning anything is inadvisable, particularly in Brisbane.

A few minutes after the Devil left, the phone rang.

I picked up the receiver. "Hello."

"We know about you," the voice on the other end of the line said.

"Who is this?"

"It's late, so I'll cut to the chase. I represent the Queensland Writers Anti-Devil Collective. We're frightened you might get involved with the Devil. He's not a nice character. Let me just say it's not in your interest to listen to him."

"And why might that be?"

"Good heavens, man, he's the Devil." There was a long sigh. "Look, all the best Brisbane writers are working with him these days. His ideas are commercial, *and* innovative, *and* classy, definitely classy. He makes the big bucks. It's the sort of money you can only dream about and . . . "

"Is this the Devil?" I asked.

There was another sigh. "Of course not, I'm just a concerned member of QWAC."

I looked down at the little screen on my phone. "I recognise your voice, and the caller ID shows it's your number. What kind of reverse psychology bullshit are you trying to pull?"

The line went dead.

I ran to the window just in time to see the Devil's living room light go out.

Fact 19: The Devil never admits that he has made a mistake, and he has been known to hold a grudge.

The next morning, I kissed my wife before she went to work, then walked down to the coffee shop, where I liked to prepare for the day's writing by drinking lots of coffee and looking all writerly.

The Devil was there, drinking a latte. There were three empty sugar packets beside the glass. He studiously ignored me.

So I ignored him.

Afterwards, I went to the hardware store, bought some bars for the windows and installed them by mid afternoon. Then, with a sense of accomplishment, I sat down and wrote. It didn't come easily, but it came, one slow word at a time.

That night, I woke to the Devil's face peering through the barred window. He hissed at me, snuck away, and rocked my roof.

The Devil isn't that bad. The other day, when I couldn't take my dog for a walk, he offered to do it for me, which I thought was nice.

—From: *People and the Devil*

(A Toowong Community Newsletter)

After the bars, things were definitely cool between him and me. He'd hide whenever I walked past his house, only a slight shiver of the curtains indicating he was there. He'd glare at me in the coffee shop and, if I'd just arrived, he'd get up and, grumbling all the way, leave. Which put me in the shop's bad books, because the Devil's a good tipper.

I gave up on writing about the Devil and started writing television. When the first episode of the show I was writing for aired, we had the Devil over for drinks. He laughed in all the right places and dabbed at his eyes with a handkerchief when it was likewise appropriate.

As the credits rolled, he smiled at me. "Very entertaining. A bit disjointed, but I trust that was the Direction."

"Of course," I said. "Another beer?"

He nodded. "Now that we're friends again, how about you remove those bars in your windows?"

"Just you keep drinking," I said.

THE DEAL

Gary Kemble

It was a problem of scale. In the humidicrib, the baby was dwarfed by the IV lines, heart monitors, and the oxygen tube taped to her nose. When Lucy had pushed their daughter out, screaming in pain and triumph, he'd thought maybe everything would be okay, maybe they'd got the dates mixed up. But ten weeks was too much; the assessment confirmed by the nursing staff rushing in with the resuscitation table, and the obstetrician ignoring the mother to concentrate on keeping this beautiful baby girl alive.

Mark reached in and stroked her tiny hand. Sarah Melissa Sullivan didn't move, save for the minute quavering rise and fall of her chest.

"Life's a bitch, isn't it?" a voice said.

Mark turned, ready for anger. But when he saw the man's face there was no trace of sarcasm in it. He was around forty, but a rough forty; there were deep laugh lines around his eyes and mouth. He looked as though he hadn't slept in a day or two, and Mark knew exactly how he felt. The man was wearing a faded AC/DC t-shirt, an open flannelette shirt and jeans that looked as though they could stand up by themselves. Mark expected him to smell, especially in this sterile environment, but all he caught was the faint, comforting scent of freshly cut hay.

He extended a hand. "Fergus. Fergus O'Brien."

"Mark Sullivan."

His grip was firm and dry. Mark noted the blurred tattoo between his thumb and forefinger—an equilateral triangle—and stared a moment too long.

"Misspent youth," Fergus said, and Mark waved it away.

"Almost got myself one once," Mark said, "but I'd spent all my money on piss."

Fergus looked past him to the humidicrib. "She's pretty," he said.

"Yeah. Sarah Melissa."

"Hello, Sarah."

Mark felt the heckles rising on his back, a protective instinct he put down to being tired and grumpy. He wished he hadn't told this man her name. A nurse passed in the hallway. Mark looked up at the walls, covered in tributes—coloured cardboard, photos, little notes in glitter pen—chronicling the lives of the residents of the Neonatal Intensive Care unit. Not all the stories had happy endings. Mark felt tears stinging his eyes, anger flaring. Why Sarah? Why the fuck Sarah?

"It's not fair, is it," Fergus said, staring down at Sarah Melissa, "that some should live and others die?"

Mark felt violated, as though the man had snatched the thought from his mind.

"I'd better get back to my wife," he said, walking out into the corridor.

Fergus grabbed Mark's wrist, his grip like a fleshy manacle. "She'll be asleep a while longer. Let her rest."

Mark wanted to ask how he knew that, but Fergus was already moving on, shoving something into his hands. Mark looked down, instantly recognising the black cover: his first novel, the best seller. The one he'd been living off these past six years.

"Could you sign this for me?" Fergus said.

Mark stared at the cover—*Chic ah Bunnah—the Devil*

Men—swamped by a mix of emotions: Anger that Fergus had even asked, while these babies struggled for life just metres away; pride that people still wanted his autograph six years on; self-loathing, as he took the pen.

"Fergus, wasn't it?" he said.

Fergus nodded. The book was yellow and dog-eared—a first edition. It was always *The Devil Men*, even though he'd written two novels since then. Mark scribbled on the cover page and Fergus grinned, taking the book and shoving it in his hessian knapsack.

"Thanks. Can I buy you a drink—some barely digestible coffee, perhaps?"

Mark shook his head. "I really do have to get going," he said, pushing past Fergus. "It was nice meeting you."

Nice. And unsettling in a way he couldn't quite define. An elevator door opened and Mark ran for it. Julie was on the maternity ward now, but Mark didn't want to lead Fergus anywhere near her. He entered. The door slid shut. Mark breathed a sigh of relief.

When the doors opened, he strode out into the hospital's airy lobby. Most of the lights were out. Outside, the cancer patients were enjoying their evening smoke. Cigarette in one hand, IV line in the other. He forced himself to walk calmly through the lobby and past the smokers. Why should he run? But as he passed the fire escape door, it burst open and Fergus staggered out, panting.

"Will you just listen to what I have to say?"

Mark ignored him, striding down the walkway towards the multi-storey car park.

Weak yellow light reflected dully on grease-stained concrete. The car park was nearly empty.

"Stay away from me," Mark yelled, over his shoulder. He pulled out his car keys and clicked the button. The orange flashers of his luxury sedan blinked twice.

"Will you just LISTEN!"

At first, Mark thought he'd been blinded. A blow to the back of the head perhaps. But now, as he stood in darkness, he thought a nervous breakdown seemed more likely. All the lights had gone off, simultaneously. The dome light in his car, the yellow car park lights. He turned, orienting himself by placing a hand on the roof of his car. Outside, the hospital was dark, even though it must've had a generator of some description. The streetlights were out, the buildings across the way were dark, as was the service station. Brisbane was dark. Maybe the whole world was dark. And although Mark couldn't see his hand in front of his face, he knew Fergus was grinning.

"Now I've got your attention, can you give me a lift home?"

Home was an East Brisbane boarding house of mouldy grey fibro, with an ancient mango tree scraping its rusty corrugated iron roof. A sign out the front proclaimed: ROOMS AVAILABLE—MEN ONLY.

Fergus invited Mark in. In a daze, Mark followed Fergus past the leering alcoholics and drug addicts, to a room at the back of the house. It was sparsely furnished, with a tattered map of Brisbane tacked to the wall.

"My real name isn't Fergus," Fergus said.

"Really?"

"No. It's Lucifer."

Mark laughed. He didn't know what else to do. "As in . . . "

"As in Satan, the Devil, Beelzebub if you're more of an Old Testament kind of guy."

Mark tried laughing again, but it came out as a wheeze. He suddenly found he couldn't speak.

"I want you to teach me to write. In exchange for saving your daughter."

Mark reeled back and rolled forwards with his right fist, just as he'd been taught in his childhood taekwon do lessons. He felt the sickening jolt of the impact. Fergus's head snapped back. When it lolled forwards again, bright red blood pumped out of his nose and across his grin.

"Nice one. I still want your help."

Mark shook his head. It was the first time he'd ever really hit someone. His hand hurt, maybe he'd broken a bone. He felt exhausted.

"Can't you just magick something up?" he asked with venom in his voice.

"I could possess another mind—make it do my bidding. But it's not the same. I can't control their creativity, their imagination. That thing, the lights in the car park, a mere parlour trick. Now what you have—that's *real* talent."

"But why would *you* even want to write?"

Fergus shrugged. "I've existed for eternity. I achieved sentience the same time homo sapiens did. And you know what?"

"No."

"It's *boring*. Boring, boring, boring. A butterfly flaps its wings, a tidal wave hits Tokyo. I sneeze, some guy decides to fly a plane into the World Trade Centre. It's boring. I want to *create*."

Mark had switched off his disbelief, because it wasn't helping. He was trying to reason with the Devil. "I wouldn't have thought saving a baby's life was exactly within your realm of responsibility," he said.

"It's a little more complicated than that," Fergus said. "It's Yin and Yang, black and white. It's karma, baby. Everything has to balance out. I *can* make your child live, but I need to make someone else's die. That's the way yours gets a chance at life."

"No," Mark said. But he was already clinging onto the hope, hating himself for it, rationalising it. The baby's room still smelt of damp paint. He thought of Jane, the time they'd spent poring over the baby book, reading about how big the baby was, what it was doing inside her womb. They were going to be such good parents. Why did Sarah have any less right to life than any of those other babies?

"No," Mark said, and walked out.

Twelve hours later he was back. He went home, tossed and turned for a couple of hours, returning to the hospital as the sun rose over Brisbane. It was another beautiful day in the Sunshine State. Things were less bright in the ICU.

Jane was sitting with the baby, tears streaming down her face. Sarah had taken a turn for the worse.

And so, he found himself back at the East Brisbane boarding house. Like any deal, the conditions were carefully laid out. Fergus wanted a series of exercises, which would lead to the completion of a single short story.

"When I type 'The End', the deal is complete. A child will die, though not your own," Fergus said.

Mark nodded, and they shook hands.

"Show me where you work," he said.

Word by word. Line by line. It's what Mark told the fans when they asked how he came up with his stories. But it was more than that. There was something secret about it too, something even he didn't understand. He never realised how little he knew about his craft until he started teaching Fergus.

And little by little, Sarah Melissa Sullivan climbed out of the dark well she'd been drowning in. As Fergus clacked away on his crusty Olivetti, Sarah edged through those crucial ten weeks.

But as one thing slipped into place, another fell apart. Joshua, another premmie, was descending into the darkness. Every day, Mark approached the ICU hoping Joshua's parents weren't there but, of course, they were. He wondered if they ate, or slept. Their vigil was like a war of attrition. He pretended Sarah wasn't doing that well, for their benefit. Each visit, they looked a little older, but no wiser.

Jane was getting suspicious; the benefit of the doubt evaporating as the days and weeks slipped by. What had he been doing with his time? Lies piled on top of lies. *I've just got to pop out for something to eat.*

There's an appointment with my agent—it's been locked in for months. Dad phoned—he needs a hand with the Commodore—she's running rough again. She thought Mark was having an affair, driven away by the stress into the arms of the bimbos that flocked around him at the book launches. And, in a way, she was right—an affair was more about lies and guilt than sex.

Guilt. For Joshua and his parents, the young couple with the sunken eyes. For his wife. For his tiny child. On the really dark days, he told himself that one day he would confide in his wife and they'd laugh about it—laugh at the fact Mark believed a deal with the Devil had saved his daughter's life. How Faustian! That thought soothed him like lanolin on sunburn. Deep down, he knew he could never tell his wife he'd traded another child's life for their daughter's. It was the sort of thing he might one day convince himself was a nightmare—if he was lucky—but he would never forget.

The most shameful thing was the savage glee he took from it. Fergus was a fast learner. He tackled the theory like a rugby league front rower and devoured the recommended reading like a hungry crocodile. Fergus's writing was still very derivative, but he was quickly developing his own style. And it was frightening—a weave of imagery and subtle plot lines that sucked you in, made you forget who you were, where you were. As Mark watched his protégé hone his skills, he imagined what it must have felt like to work on the first atomic bomb at Los Alamos.

Word by word, line by line, the deal with the Devil went on.

As Mark drove into the hospital, he was already constructing the lies that would get him to his next meeting with Fergus. His satanic student was going to phone him on the mobile, pretending to be a friend whose car had broken down and needed a lift. Today was *the* day: Fergus was going to show him his completed short story. Mark's belly tingled with anticipation.

He wasn't thinking of Sarah, or his wife, or poor Joshua when he walked into the ICU, waving to a nurse on the way through—the staff had become like a second family these past eight weeks—instead, he was thinking of Fergus's story.

Mark pushed through the double doors, at first thinking the crowd of people he saw were gathered around Sarah's humidicrib. He thought he'd been double-crossed, that Fergus was abandoning them now he'd mastered another dark art. A nurse pushed past him, tearing an implement out of its sterile packaging as she rushed by.

"Excuse me," she said, elbowing him into the corner of the room.

Sarah's humidicrib was empty and Mark felt his pulse throbbing thickly in his throat. Then he saw Jane nursing Sarah to her chest. On the other side of the room were Joshua's parents. His father was slack-faced, pasty. His mother was clutching her eyes as though blocking out the sight to make this horror go away. The crowd of bodies shuffled around for a moment and Mark saw the resuscitation table—Joshua laid out on its surface, lit from above by heating elements. He looked so stark under that light, so fragile. Doctors and nurses handling tiny implements moved frantically to save his tiny life.

"Mark?"

He turned to see Jane and clutched her hand, looking down in amazement at their own baby, out of the humidicrib for the first time. He wanted to ask Jane how this had come to be, but now wasn't the time or the place.

His phone rang in his pocket, vibrating. The obstetrician turned awkwardly, staring at him. The phone trilled again.

"Get that thing out of here!"

But Mark was already moving, shaking off Jane's hand, through the double doors, into the lobby, ignoring the frowns.

"Call it off!" Mark said into the mobile.

"Mark?"

Fergus was grinning, he could tell.

"I don't want any part of this," Mark said. "Call it off."

"I'm at a phone box. We'd better talk about this face to face."

"Whatever. Just don't do anything until I get there. Fergus? Fergus!"
The line was dead.

"Mark?"

Jane was at his shoulder, holding their daughter. It would have been
so easy to just stay there, cry into her shoulder, just let it all unfold.
He'd come so far.

"I have to do something," he said.

He ran, ignoring her angry questions at his back.

Every red light was eternity.

Fergus was waiting for him, sitting in the sun on the front steps, grinning again. In his hand, a sheaf of paper glowed brilliantly in the
sunlight.

Mark pushed open the gate so hard that the rusted hinges snapped,
and the gate fell away into the weeds behind it.

"I don't want any part of this," he yelled, rushing up the steps and
grabbing Fergus by the collar. He thrust him against the door frame.
The wood shuddered and Fergus flopped like a rag doll, but he didn't
stop grinning. Mark dropped him and he landed on his feet, stumbling
down into the garden.

"It's too late," Fergus said.

Mark hit him hard. Fergus's head cracked to the side. The grin
disappeared for a moment. Fergus spat two teeth and a wad of blood
into the overgrown grass.

"It's still too late," Fergus said. "I've typed 'The End'."

"No, you're not finished. It's a first draft. Just a first draft. You still
need me."

Fergus shrugged, offering the sheaf of paper. "That wasn't the
agreement. 'The End' was the agreement. Besides it's perfect now; I
don't need you anymore."

Mark snatched the story from him. His eyes scanned the lines of type. It was good. He could tell that, even though he was in no state to write a critique.

"Keep it," Fergus said, walking back into the boarding house. "I've got it all up here." He tapped the side of his head.

Mark would've killed him, had he a weapon, had it been possible to kill the Devil. As it was, he stood there in the garden for a few moments, breathing heavily. He told himself he'd burn the story, but he knew he'd read it first. This was his child, after all, just as much as Sarah was. He flicked through to the final page. Halfway down, centred: TEH END.

He read the last page again, the typo catching his eye. Hope surged.

Mark was prepared for yelling when he got back to the hospital. He felt he deserved it. But there must've been something in his face, because when he saw Jane waiting outside intensive care, Sarah still clutched to her chest, she simply came to him, offering him the tiny baby wrapped in white.

"Would you like to hold your daughter?" she said.

Mark broke down, sobs jerking out of his mouth, tears rolling down his cheeks. He slumped against the wall, legs buckling. Jane sat down beside him.

He took Sarah, cradling her in his arms, staring down at her even though he couldn't see her through the tears. She cried, like a tiny outboard motor, and he laughed. He wiped his cheeks, sniffed.

The door to the ICU opened. Joshua's dad walked out. Mark didn't think he'd be able to look him in the eye, but he found he couldn't look away.

"I'm sorry," Mark said.

"Huh?" He stopped, head tilted slightly to one side.

"About Joshua. I'm sorry."

A flicker of a smile touched one corner of his mouth. "He's still hanging in there," he said. "It was close, but he's still hanging in there."

He smiled more broadly now, and Mark returned the gesture, grinning until he was crying with joy.

THE PLURIPOTENTIARY

Chris Lynch

I

The smiling Greek nude etched into the glass matched the logo on the card in my hand. I pushed the door open and found myself in a small, dimly lit room. It was air-conditioned and carpeted. To the left, there were a few chairs and a coffee table with magazines stacked neatly upon it. Directly opposite was a reception desk, the sort that had one of those high counters that made it easy to sign cheques and credit card slips on. Beyond it, was another door that no doubt led to the main office. Except for several pieces of surreal art on the walls, the place had the feel of a doctor's waiting room.

There was no one in sight. I walked over to a large poster that depicted another naked figure. It was promotional copy: *We completely cure creative dysfunction, with the full protection of our no-questions-asked money-back guarantee. Muse, the choice of Nobel laureates.*

"Good afternoon."

I turned, startled.

"Can I help you, sir?"

I realised that the high-pitched voice was coming from the reception desk. I moved closer and peered over the top. A tiny blonde woman in a red dress was seated before an LCD screen. She smiled at me.

"Can I help you?" she asked again.

"I hope so," I said affably. "My name's Phil Jackson. I'm a writer with *The Courier-Mail*. I'm doing a story on Muse."

Her pencilled eyebrows frowned slightly. "We don't usually talk to journalists. But just a moment, I'll call Dr Vishnevski." She picked up the receiver and pressed a number, tilting her head and playing with her earring while she waited. Her arched neck was quite beautiful, flowing down into a plunging neckline.

"You've got a Phil Jackson here, from *The Courier-Mail*." She glanced up at me and smiled again. "Yes, that's right." She put the phone down. "If you'd like to take a seat, Mr Jackson, Dr Vishnevski will see you in a minute."

"Thank you," I said warmly. It's always a good idea to make friends with the secretary.

"Not at all." She gave me another smile.

I barely had time to sit down before Dr Vishnevski breezed in. He was a large man, tall and solid, with grey eyes. He had a closely cropped salt-and-pepper beard and was dressed in a pristine white coat.

"Mr Jackson, Michael Vishnevski." He shook my hand firmly.

"A pleasure," I said.

"Did you have much trouble finding us?" His accent was mild and hard to place. East European?

"A little," I replied. "It's not an easy place to find, even for a journalist."

He smiled modestly. "We try to avoid the corporate look, which is why we're a little out of the way." He gestured to the doorway. "Shall we?"

I nodded.

"Warm outside?" he asked, guiding me into his office.

"Very," I replied.

He sat down in a plush leather chair, and motioned for me to take the seat opposite. "Can I get you something to drink? Ice water, coffee?"

"No, I'm fine thanks."

"Right. So, what can I do for you, Mr Jackson?"

"Phil's fine. I'm interested in interviewing you for an article, perhaps even a feature. Muse is an intriguing organization, but I confess I've found very little information on you."

"Our clientele are generally very discerning, very private individuals. We prefer to keep a low profile. As a rule, we don't do interviews with the media."

"I see. Are there any circumstances in which you'd be prepared to make an exception?"

Dr Vishnevski gazed at me levelly for a moment. "We choose our clients very carefully, Mr Jackson," he said, avoiding my question. "Not all applications for treatment are successful and, as you might expect, we get a lot of applications."

"I'm sure you do."

"Do you freelance at all?"

I cocked my head. "I have done. Why?"

"*The Courier-Mail* isn't, shall we say, our target audience. But, if you could find a more specialised publication willing to do a feature story, I think we'd be very open to that, provided that you underwent the treatment yourself. To give the readers a complete picture of the experience."

"I see," I said noncommittally. "What makes you think I'm creatively dysfunctional?"

Dr Vishnevski smiled. "Well, no offence, Mr Jackson," he said, eyeing my hairline, "but your age. When you get as old as we are, creativity inevitably slows, in quantity of output if not in quality. The treatment's simple and perfectly routine—I've had it done myself. It requires only an overnight stay in our clinic." He paused. "We would, of course, significantly reduce our fees," he added smoothly, stroking his beard. "So, are you interested?"

"I'd need to know a little more about the treatment first. Could you explain it, in general terms—off the record?"

He smiled again. "Certainly."

II

Purple blossoms are again heralding the end of winter and the advent of examinations for university students all over Brisbane.

The jacarandas are blooming and as usual students are the only ones unhappy to see the arrival of purple spring.

The streets of Brisbane are once again paved with mauve droppings . . .

I was trying to find a new angle to this tired seasonal story, and failing miserably. Admittedly, I wasn't trying very hard, but it was depressing nonetheless. Seeking inspiration (and photos of attractive young women carrying books) I ventured down to the university.

It was an unusually hot September morning, the hottest in over a century, one of those days commonly taken by garrulous strangers to be an omen of a blistering summer. I wandered across the lawn of the Great Court, looking for a suitable group of students—fresh-faced, colourfully dressed, preferably ethnically mixed. A few crows were picking over some rubbish, and their cawing echoed off the sandstone buildings.

A young man approached me. He was a pale, weedy fellow dressed completely in black and wearing large glasses. Oddly, given the heat, he wasn't sweating at all.

"Phil Jackson," he said. It wasn't a question.

"Yes," I said guardedly. "Can I help you?"

He smiled. "I hope so."

Abruptly, the crows fell silent. I looked around. Except for the man before me, not a single person was moving.

"Who are you?" I asked.

"I'm Satan," he said, "and I'd like to make you an offer."

III

I went down to the newspaper's morgue to look for jacarandas. An annual story, there were bound to be dozens of clippings in the newspaper archives. I'm not sure why I bothered; after thirty years in the business, I could have written it in the time it took me to walk down the stairs to the basement.

But lately I'd become dissatisfied with my copy—and so, it seemed, had my editor, to have given me an assignment like this on my first day back from my break. Not exactly a story calling for my incisive investigative skills. It was a slow news day, I told myself. And all the cadets were out.

Since the Muse story, I'd grown more and more restless. There had to be something more to life than this endless procession of copy, the same people writing the same stories about the same people, using the same words, day after day, week after week.

The scar from the operation had almost completely healed, and was barely visible beneath my slowly re-sprouting hair. Dr Vishnevski had said I should anticipate results from the stem cells within six to eight weeks, so I was keen to apply my brain to a problem requiring a creative solution. The jacaranda story seemed a good test. If I could write something interesting about examinations and spring blossoms, I'd consider the operation a complete success.

As expected, I found plenty of previous articles. I laid them out on a table and began flicking through them. Predictably, they were all soporific. "The purple blossoms of Brisbane are once again heralding blah blah blah . . . " What a load of shit.

A sharp stabbing pain suddenly hit me in the head. The newsprint blurred and faded into darkness. As I put my hand up to my temple, I felt myself slide off the chair. I was unconscious before I hit the floor.

IV

The devil smiled, tucking an auburn tress behind a perfect ear.

"I'm not asking you to trust me. I am, after all, the Prince of Darkness. I'm merely putting forward a proposition. You can take it or leave it." She leaned back and sipped her cocktail.

"No writer's block?" I pressed.

"No writer's block."

"I still don't get how it works."

"It has to do with quantum organics and the many-worlds."

"Quantum organics?"

"I thought you'd say that. I don't suppose you've heard of Pythagoras's Cat?" The devil sighed. "It's technical. To tell you the truth I'm not really sure how it works exactly. I have demons who take care of the details."

"No offence, but I get worried when Satan brushes over the details. I've read stories. What are you trying to say?"

"I'm saying that, should you accept my offer, all universes in which you are not a successful writer—an infinite number—will cease to exist. The wave function, the entire set of possibilities, will be collapsed to a smaller set. A better one."

"You're suggesting I annihilate an infinite number of souls in exchange for, what, the Nobel Prize for Literature?" I contemplated the bourbon before me, and resisted the urge to down the entire glass.

"Not at all," she said briskly, her cherubic face lighting up as she lit another cigarette. "Remember that the soul is a superposition of the countless decisions made by every version of a person in the multiverse. And every time a decision is made, the universe splits."

"So?"

"So, for every universe that is collapsed, there are billions of other universes which are exactly the same, in every respect, except that you are successful as a writer."

"How is that possible? How could the universes in which I'm unsuccessful be exactly the same as the ones in which I'm successful? What about all the repercussions from my success?"

"Like what?"

"I don't know. All sorts of things. Like the ant I step on at a writers' festival I'm invited to as a guest speaker."

"What makes you think that someone else doesn't step on the ant? In many universes it's probably the very writer who replaced you as speaker who steps on it, at precisely the same time as you would. In other universes, of course, you still step on it; you're just not a guest speaker at the festival."

"But there must be an infinite number of universes in which the ant isn't squashed."

"Yes. But don't forget that in an infinite number of those universes, the writer who fails to step on the ant is you."

"There must be *some* differences," I insisted, "differences that matter."

"Oh, there are minor physical differences," Satan conceded breezily, crossing her pudgy legs and flicking ash into the bar ashtray. "When you remove an infinite number of universes from the multiverse, of course something must be lost. And some information is lost. But what you must understand is that while each universe physically differs, if only by a single atom, most are *morally equivalent*. And that's all that matters."

I rubbed sweat from my sandy eyes. "What do you mean, 'morally equivalent'?"

The devil puffed her cigarette enthusiastically. "Okay, I've got a good example. Just now you rubbed your eyes, right? Well, in another universe, you didn't. You kept looking at your drink."

"I thought we were outside Time," I said, gesturing at the mannequins frozen in mid-blink around us.

"Yes, well, I mean *normally*, when you're not talking to the devil." She waved the cigarette. "Look, the point is, the vast majority of decisions that you're making every minute of every day are not significant in the grand moral scheme, and have no long-term consequences."

I drank the bourbon.

V

The doctor stroked his beard uneasily.

"I've said it often enough to other patients, but for once there really *is* no easy way to tell you this," he said. He looked again at the sheaf of scans before him and abruptly pushed them across his desk to me.

It took me a few moments to work out what I was looking at. Shades of grey on black suddenly snapped into focus. In the centre burned a strange white star. My hands clenched the plastic slides.

"I've got a tumour." I'd half-expected it, but it was still a shock.

"In a manner of speaking," he said. His voice was distant.

"What do you mean?"

"Have a look at the next one."

I stared at the image, frozen. Incredulous. "Is this real?"

"As far as we can tell. Short of drilling into your skull again."

I shuffled through the scans, searching for a piece of sanity. "This is impossible. There must be some mistake." I was incapable of anything but clichés.

"That would be the most reasonable explanation, yes. But as you're well aware, we've done dozens of tests. We've imaged your brain in as many different ways as we can."

"Some kind of error . . ."

"No. It shows up on all the machines. Besides . . . "

"A tumour. Just an unusual tumour." I couldn't take my eyes off it.

"Tumours don't have . . . " He stopped. "They aren't . . . differentiated to that degree."

"How big is it?"

"About the size of your thumb."

"Jesus Christ. How long has it been in there?"

"I don't know. It looks about eight weeks old to me, but I'm a neurologist, not an obstetrician."

"It's alive?"

"Apparently so."

I attempted to digest this piece of information. "Why has it got a tail?" For some reason it seemed important.

"All of them do at the beginning. That's normal."

"I fail to see what's normal about this."

"Of course," he said quickly. "I just meant . . . "

"What are these little bumps on the—near the top? Are they normal as well?"

"No. We're not sure what they are."

Silence.

"You're telling me I have a foetus growing in my head," I said flatly. The doctor looked at me directly for the first time since I'd entered the room.

"Yes."

"The operation I had, it caused this?"

"I don't know, Phil, I really don't. There's just no precedent for this, and I have no idea what they put in your head. It's certainly plausible. From what you've said they told you, the treatment sounds very experimental. If they harvested the cells from an embryo, perhaps a totipotent ... well, as I say, I don't know."

"Dr Vishnevski said they isolated pluripotent stem cells from my blood. That's one of the reasons he said it was so safe."

"Yes, well that's the other thing: we haven't been able to find any record of a Dr Vishnevski in the country, let alone the state—either past or present."

A chill ran down my spine. "What about the card I gave you, with the address?"

"I went there myself on the way home last night. The place was empty; there was a 'For Lease' sign out the front." The doctor shrugged. "I've notified the police, but I'm afraid 'Muse Ltd' has vanished."

VI

"So in exchange I have to give you my soul?" My mind teemed with a trillion thoughts, all tussling to express themselves at once like chickens in a titanic barn.

"Not at all," she said. The devil leant her frail bird-like carcass on her loaded shopping trolley. "I'm asking for something much, much less. In exchange for collapsing all universes in which you are a failure, you will give me one of the infinite versions of you that is successful."

"In other words, a piece of my soul," I replied. I was still puzzled by what this had to do with Einstein's cat.

"An infinitesimally small piece," she allowed.

"Little consolation for the poor bastard who gets chosen," I muttered. My eyes fell to the can of fish in my hand. I put it back on the shelf.

"Well, yes," she agreed good-humouredly. "But that's life, isn't it? At least he'll know that an infinite number of you are enjoying the success that is your due."

"What are you going to do with him?" I inquired. "Torture him forever?"

The devil laughed in a lovely lilting voice, like an opera singer being tickled by a conductor. "Please. I have far better things to do with my eternity, I assure you." She brushed a vagrant wisp of snowy white hair from in front of her chocolate brown eyes. In her sparkling clean cotton dress, she looked every bit the wise benevolent fairy godmother.

"So, what do you want with him?" I asked again, a little tetchily. It's not every day that Satan approaches you in the supermarket.

"To be honest, I don't know; I haven't decided yet. Perhaps I'll need the services of a writer one day," she mused with a smile. "You certainly don't need to bother with all that medieval imagery."

A thought suddenly occurred to me: "If I agree, all unsuccessful versions of me will instantly cease to exist, right?"

"Yes, that's right," she agreed.

"So, what if I turn out to be a terrible writer?" I blurted. "I'd be agreeing to terminate myself." I contemplated the multitudinous cans of fish before me.

"Are you a terrible writer?" The corners of her mouth twitched suddenly like she was being violently electrocuted, but only slightly, and she arched an eyebrow.

"Well, no, but . . . "

"It doesn't matter," she said cutting me off. "In your future, there are successful writers. In an infinite universe, anything is possible. You won't notice any change."

She reached into her trolley and dexterously pulled out a can of soft drink in one swift movement, like an octogenarian octopus on speed. "Sprite?" she asked.

I shook my head.

"Suit yourself," she said, opening it with a loud 'pshht' and sipping it daintily.

I stared at the can and was struck suddenly by another thought. "If you're in every universe, offering every version of everyone their heart's desire, doesn't that make you omnipresent, omniscient and omnipotent?"

The devil laughed easily. "Not quite. I am part of God's plan. God created the firmament; I help to shape it. But I am merely a messenger.

The Angel of Choice. That's why people hate me. They fear choice, because with it comes responsibility. So they blame me for their decisions instead."

She took another sip of Sprite. "It's amazing, the unintended consequences of choice. Did you know that there are countless timelines in which World War II victory turns on which shade of green Churchill's underpants are one day in 1943? If it's lime, even Patton can't avoid an Allied defeat."

"Is this relevant?" I asked. I was fast losing my patience for gasbagging in the aisles with this loquacious and quite frankly long-winded old lady.

"Suit yourself. I find it fascinating. I'm a real student of history." She chuckled like a boiling kettle. "The things I could tell you about Kim Jong-il."

"Side-splitting, no doubt."

Her smile faded. "In my job you get your laughs where you can, I assure you." She looked away. "Everything that is possible is. That includes all kinds of depravities. Entire universes of sickness and horror. I shudder just thinking of it."

She seemed very small all of a sudden, and I almost gave her a comforting hug before I remembered she was Satan. Suddenly, yet another thought struck me. "So what happens when everyone has made their choice," I asked, "about which versions of themselves they want collapsed?"

"You're full of questions today, aren't you?" She gave me a long, penetrating look, pregnant with hidden cryptic meanings. "Essentially the multiverse wave function is in a state of collapse towards a world in which all conscious beings have chosen to be," she replied at last.

"When will that happen?" I asked, adroitly manoeuvring my trolley around the stationary housewife next to us. I might as well get something out of this, I thought.

"It's going to take a while," the devil conceded.

VII

"I want you to cut it out. Now."

The doctor shifted in his chair. "I'm not sure that's a good idea," he said.

"Why not?"

He pulled on his beard. "We're not sure if it's malignant. Until we do, the best course of action is to continue gathering information."

"You're joking. Look, this isn't a tumour we're talking about—I have a fucking foetus growing in my head."

"I appreciate your concern, Phil. Have you considered alternatives to abortion?"

"What?"

"As you say, this isn't a tumour. As far as we can tell, it's a living human being. Don't you wonder who it is?"

I stared at him. "Look, I wonder all sorts of things, but one thing I do know: a foetus gets a lot bloody bigger than my head."

"You'd be surprised. The technology's catching up extremely fast. Premmies are now viable even at . . . "

"I. Don't. Care." My voice was shaking. "I want it out. Out of my goddamn head. Simple as that."

VIII

"Yes, I think I understand," the psychiatrist said seriously. "I've read a bit about quantum theory. So what did you say then?"

"I refused."

He made a note in his book. "Why?" he asked, looking up.

"It seemed too good to be true. Besides, what if I turned out to be one of the unsuccessful ones? I'd be committing suicide."

He made another note. "Quite. And what did the devil say when you refused?"

"He didn't seem bothered at all. I asked him why, and he shrugged. He said: 'You've chosen to decline, but all it takes is for me to find one of you who'll accept, and it's done. Finding one desperate writer is really only a question of probabilities. And in an infinite universe, the probability is always one.'" I paused, rubbing my temple.

"That's it?" he asked.

"Yeah. Everything started moving again, and he walked off."

"You didn't try to follow him?"

"Yeah, I did. But it wasn't him anymore."

"How do you know?"

"He just went over to a table and started playing blackjack again. I followed him anyway, but eventually he talked to security and they asked me to leave."

The psychiatrist nodded thoughtfully, pursing his lips. He made a few more notes. "Mmmn," he said after a moment. "Okay, Phil, I'm going to up your medication a little. See if that doesn't have an effect."

IX

I opened my eyes. The sunlight had barely shifted; I'd only dozed for a few minutes. I tried to move my head, and groaned.

I heard murmuring outside the door, and then the doctor came in. I could tell from her voice it was the overly cheerful one.

"Good morning, Mr Jackson! How are we this morning? Feeling any better?"

"No."

"I have some good news. You'll be happy to know we've decided to operate."

"Why?" They'd put it off for nearly two weeks now.

"It's . . . not responding to the therapy as well as we'd like, so we've decided to go for surgery."

"What do you mean, not responding?"

There was a pause. "Do you remember those two little extra buds on the foetus?" she asked evenly.

"What about them?"

"They're developing."

X

"And so," I concluded gravely, "if the universe *is* a cosmic joke, it is, at the very least, one we can laugh at too." I took off my horn-rimmed glasses with both hands and smiled humbly as the audience in the Great Hall rose as one to applaud my Nobel lecture.

It felt good.

The congratulations went on well into the night. Diane still had jetlag, so after a few hours she left and went back to the hotel. The recognition of my work was, of course, gratifying, but I eventually became weary of all the sycophants and publishers. Finally managing to extricate myself, I said farewell and strode with long, purposeful strides out into the chilly night.

Outside it was quiet and still. The snow lay thick on the ground, a palimpsest of footprints. I turned up the collar of my coat, but I didn't really mind the cold; it was a pleasant change from the unusual heat of the summer back in Brisbane. If only the Americans would sign Kyoto, I thought. I crunched down the steps towards the road.

"Mr Jackson!" A male voice. I turned. An old man hurried down the stairs after me. There was something odd about the fellow, but I couldn't quite put my finger on it. Probably just the accent, I thought. Or maybe the smile.

"I suppose you want my autograph?"

He seemed surprised. "Why, yes, as a matter of fact I do."

I pulled out my gold fountain pen, a gift from my father-in-law. "Where?" I asked, tired and a little impatient to get back to the hotel to Diane, who was no doubt patiently waiting up for me.

"Just here. Thank you, you're very kind."

I managed a gracious smile for the man. "Not at all. My pleasure."

The old man smirked. I checked for my wallet, suddenly uneasy. It was still there, so I hailed a cab and disappeared into the Stockholm night.

It had been the best day of my life.

XI

"Why me?"

"Ah, yes. The eternal question." The surgeon's patrician features moved into view again. "I've often wondered that myself, believe me."

"What you ... do with me?" I asked. I was trapped in the straps and clamps of the surgical table, my face was numb from the drugs, but I could still slur my words.

The devil tilted the mirror slightly so I could see my open braincase. A red sac was partially embedded in the right hemisphere. "Incredible, isn't it? To think that these few pounds of flesh are a decision-making machine capable of producing the great art and science of the world. It's fascinating."

"What you do with me?" I repeated. My vision blurred as tears welled up. I couldn't feel them on my face.

"Oh, I'm sure I'll have need of a famous writer at some point," he said, stroking his pointed beard.

"Don't understand. Not famous."

"Nonsense. You're a very successful journalist."

"Don't understand," I said, my throat clenched with fear and grief. "What's happening?"

The devil peered at me. "It's okay," he said kindly. "I haven't finished explaining." He resumed his pacing.

"So, are you clear about Schrödinger's Cat and the many-worlds?" He took my silence for assent. "Right, so essentially what I'm saying is

163

that this world, the universe we're in now, is about to become the best of all possible worlds, as determined by the collective choices of all conscious beings."

I tried to concentrate. "Humans?" I could feel the injection he'd given me taking effect; I was regaining control of my tongue.

"Yes. But also the countless individuals from other *Homo* species, a dozen chimpanzees, a couple of AIs, and even an augmented dolphin named Tuner."

"That's impossible."

"No, just unlikely. Incidentally, he decided to die young rather than face the scientists."

"No, I mean, an infinite number of universes. They can never be collapsed to a single universe."

"Really?" He sounded interested. The devil moved back beside me. "What makes you say that?"

"Because half of infinity is still infinity. You can collapse as many universes as you like and you'll still end up with an infinite number of them."

"Very perceptive of you." He seemed surprised. "You're absolutely right. Your condition appears to have done wonders for your powers of deduction."

"Then why are you smiling?"

"It's a fascinating thing. It turns out that infinity is not quite what it seems."

"What do you mean?"

"There is actually no such thing as infinity. It's absurd—useful only to mathematicians and science-fiction writers. There are numbers too large for the human mind to fathom, but nothing is infinite."

"Not even God?"

The devil grimaced. "No. But don't point it out to Him." He pulled at his beard, and resumed pacing.

"As I'm sure you're aware, I've been offering choices on an *ad hoc* basis since the Garden of Eden. I thought the same as you did for aeons—that the multiverse was infinite. It took a long time to understand that this was impossible. But by the time I realised what I could do, there were trillions and trillions of universes splitting at an exponential rate.

"So it took me a while to prune the branching multiverse down to a more manageable size. Sheer drudgery. But once I approached the problem systematically, it was only a matter of time before I succeeded. It was just a question of playing people's choices off against each other.

"Why did I do it, you ask? Well, you see, it's very simple. I'm tired of talking to the same people about the same choice, over and over and over and over and over again. And I'm sick of all the abominations God has allowed to come into existence," he continued, warming to his topic and pacing even faster. "All the pain and suffering and destruction in the multiverse makes me want to vomit. Enough aborted universes. It's time for a world of purity. A world of choice, not randomness. A world where things are made right."

The devil looked down at me. "And your little *deus ex machina*, my friend, is the key to this new world."

"What did you do to me?" I demanded.

"Nothing." He sounded offended. "I haven't touched a single hair on your head. No, the foetus is a complete anomaly." He moved behind me and peered into my head. "A miracle, in fact. Quite why it grew in you as it has is a mystery known only to God. It hasn't happened to anyone else in the multiverse."

"You didn't put it in my head?" Disbelief.

"Not at all. All I can do is offer choices. As far as I can tell it was a statistical fluke, a bizarre side effect of the stem cell treatment. It only happened in a tiny fraction of the universes in which you had the treatment. Nearly all of the embryos died, or killed you. But this one ... "

"What do you want it for?"

He eyed the red sac like an expectant mother and then looked at me in the mirror. "The Pope is wrong: the soul enters the body only as it's born."

"So?"

"It's time I had my own body."

Silence.

"Well, I think I'll let our surgeon get back to it. As we speak, the last choices are being made. I want to be in your head at the precise moment of birth, the nanosecond in which the wave function of the entire multiverse is collapsed to one final perfect solution."

"But it can't last," I said desperately, searching for a chink in his armour. "In the next instant people will make choices, and the world will begin splitting again."

Satan smiled. There was a hint of satisfaction in his deep-set eyes. "You forget: every other person in this universe accepted my offer as well. In return, all of them granted me one of their copies. Since this is about to become the only universe in existence, I am exercising my right to the last remaining version of everyone; I own their souls too. I can shape the future any way I choose."

He lifted his mask back over his face and picked up a scalpel with a tiny curved blade. "Thank you, Mr Jackson. It's been a real pleasure dealing with you."

He returned to slicing and a moment later his assistants began moving again. The surgeon asked for another set of forceps. I could see him probing my brain in the mirror.

"We're nearly there, people," he said tersely. "Get ready."

Gently—so gently!—the surgeon eased the little growth from the tangle of blood vessels, while an assistant snipped and cauterised with the efficient gestures of a hairdresser.

At last, it slipped free of the brain.

The surgeon lowered the foetus into the waiting receptacle, and it sank into clear viscosity. I could see it moving.

No sooner had the surgeon placed it in the temporary womb, than the white-robed nurse was wheeling the trolley out of the room. As she did, I glimpsed the foetus a final time, caught in the glare of the surgical lamps. It looked like an infant rodent in a flaring halo of blood. From its back, two delicate wings blossomed into the fluid.

I could have sworn its half-formed face was smiling.

THE WRITER WHO COULD HAVE BEEN DOSTOYEVSKY

Geoffrey Maloney

At about nine o'clock in the evening at the end of November, during a St Petersburg thaw, Fyodor Mikhailovich Dostoyevsky flung down his pen and swept the manuscript he had been working on to the floor. He stomped upon the papers with a bright gleam in his eyes. His heart was pounding in his ears. But never had he felt so wonderful as he did in that decisive moment. "I have beaten you," he cried as he shook his fist triumphantly at the ceiling and then at the floor. "From this day forth I shall write no more. I renounce my vocation. I win! You lose, you bastard! The pact is null and void!"

Then taking his hat and heavy coat, he abandoned his apartment and rushed down the stairs, his thoughts flying wildly: He can't touch me now. He can't get me. Oh, no, he can't. My soul is my own. He thinks he's so smart. But if I don't write, what can he do? Nothing. Absolutely nothing. Of course, he can't—And in such a rapturous joy was he that he blew raspberries to the wind and giggled gleefully, oblivious to the stares of those who bumped him on the street.

Twenty minutes later, Dostoyevsky was in the grip of his favourite passion. The roulette wheel spun. The roubles tumbled. No longer a writer; now he would be a professional gambler, the greatest the world had ever seen. He was sure of it.

The Devil came and sat next to him and said in his most cajoling voice, "Fyodor Mikhailovich, I beg you to reconsider. I beseech you. We have a deal. It is a binding pact. You *will* be a famous writer. You shall be magnificent. The world of mortal men shall bow down before your immaculate creations. God himself will sigh when he reads what you have written."

"Ah, ha, did you hear that?" Dostoyevsky said, rising from his chair and crying out loud to anyone who would listen. "This gentleman here, the one right next to me, so mild-mannered in appearance, so nicely dressed, such a charming face, with such sweet words flowing from his ruby lips—well, let me tell you, gentlemen, this is the devil in disguise. But I have my pride, gentlemen. Yes, I do, and this bastard shall not take my soul. Yes, I agreed with him once. What a fool I was. What was I thinking? But no more, no more. I have beaten him! Now spin the wheel, roll the ball. Let's get on with the game."

"Believe me, Fyodor, there are other ways to deal with this," the Devil said.

Dostoyevsky turned away. The roulette wheel spun. The roubles tumbled.

At the same time, or thereabouts, during a thunderstorm, one of Australia's most popular authors, James P. McMannis, was being interviewed live in a television studio at Mt Cootha. Outside, in typical Brisbane fashion, lightning ripped the sky apart, thunder roared and great fat slugs of rain burst upon the ground. Inside the studio, thanks to its artificial lighting, insulation and a total lack of windows, the storm could only be detected as a distant hum.

Right now, oblivious to the raging storm, the television host was saying, "You've sold over a million books in the last two years. In

Australia and overseas. You're one of our most popular writers of all time. How does that feel?"

"Well, it's all been quite wonderful," McMannis said and beamed his best very-nice smile. "I'm happy that I've been able to connect with so many people. Grateful really that people enjoy what I've been doing."

"So what do you say to your critics when they say that you've never written anything substantial, nothing that will last?" the host asked.

"Such a difficult question," McMannis said. "I don't know if anyone really knows what substantial is when it comes to writing. My work is important to the readers, as I've said before, and that's important to me, substantial. If it's long lasting, then only time will tell. I mean, I'm hardly going to compare myself to Shakespeare, but he was very popular in his time as well."

"Now it's time for my second difficult question. Your writing has been compared—very favourably, I should say—to Wilbur Smith, James Clavell and P. D. James. But was there a single point in your life where you read a particular writer that made you say, "Yes, I want to write too? If so, who was that writer?"

Such a good question, McMannis thought. He couldn't help himself. His publicist had told him never to say it, that most of his audience, his readers, wouldn't have a clue what he was talking about. But it was such a direct question and he gave an honest reflex response. He was in Brisbane after all; his hometown. "It was Dostoyevsky. He changed my life."

Outside, the lightning struck. The thunder clapped instantly; it was a direct hit. The studio shook and collapsed into darkness.

"Shit, get the lights back on," the host cried. "Aren't the back-up generators supposed to be running?"

"Off the air," somebody called out. "Totally, fucking, off the air."

McMannis sat in his chair. He could no longer see his host or the studio audience. He couldn't even see his hand as he held it up in front of his face. Around him, he could feel the studio crew stumbling about, muttering an occasional curse. The audience are being so calm, he thought. But then again, like himself, perhaps they thought it was better to remain in their seats and be silent. It *was* Brisbane. Blackouts were commonplace. He had grown up with them as a child, could remember the days when he had almost ruined his eyesight in his bedroom, out on the sleep-out, struggling to read "The Brothers Karamazov" by candlelight. His teacher had given it to him, told him it was a challenging book. He'd devoured it over several nights, reading at a voracious pace. But the time came when he told himself that even if he could write as well as Dostoyevsky, nobody would read books like that any more. Too much angst and intensity, not enough romance, mystery or swashbuckling action. No adventure.

Lost in his thoughts, it was some time before McMannis realised that he was surrounded by perfect silence. "There doesn't seem to be much chance of the lights coming back on. Are there any candles?" he asked, trying to put a merry tone into his voice.

He had expected his host to respond, but nothing came back. He listened intently. He couldn't hear a thing. Then slowly the lights did come back on—but it was an eerie light, a brownout, that seemed to shroud the studio in a smoky haze. It was only then he was aware that everybody else appeared to have departed, leaving him sitting in the guest's chair all alone. Impossible, he thought. A practical joke? But then, through the haze, he saw a man approaching. A rather dapper gent dressed in a neat black suit with a flashy red bow tie. His hair too was black, with a little grey showing at the temples, and slicked back flat across the dome of his head.

"Ah," he said, "I'm glad you're still here. Running a little late, I'm afraid. Things never seem to work out just as I'd planned. But not to worry. It is a great pleasure to make your acquaintance."

"And you are?" McMannis asked, taking his hand and feeling how hot and sweaty it was.

"Your humble servant."

"The driver who's supposed to be picking me up?" McMannis asked.

The dapper gent inclined his head to the side quickly in what may have been a nod or perhaps just a nervous twitch. "We'd best be off," he said. "There's a lull in the storm." Then he turned and walked off at a brisk pace.

McMannis rose quickly from his chair and raced after him.

They exited the studio and followed a long corridor with a decidedly downward slope to it.

"Rather odd," McMannis said, "how everybody just seems to have disappeared."

"I was watching the show," the driver said. "Your story about reading Dostoyevsky by candlelight . . . How beautiful. How touching. 'Yes,' I cried, 'yes, this is the writer I have been looking for.'"

McMannis grew a little nervous. He could not remember actually telling that story. Certainly, he had thought about it . . . but the lights had already gone out by then; he was sure of it. "I don't quite understand," he said.

"I appreciate that," the driver said, "but believe me when I tell you I am desperately in need of your assistance."

"This is very confusing," McMannis said, noticing that they were now exiting from the corridor and beginning to descend a long winding staircase. He took a few steps, then stopped. "I think you'd better tell me what this is all about."

The driver who was clearly no driver at all continued to descend. "This is an opportunity that you cannot afford to miss," he said. "This is your chance at long-lasting fame. This is the opportunity to write something that will last after your death. The world will read what you have written for centuries. Besides, did I not just tell you that I am in desperate need of your assistance? But, by all means, leave now if you wish. But forever you will be tormented and ask yourself 'what if?' Yes, right now you can leave and return to your sycophantic studio audience of well-wishers and your third rate TV host. Return to your best-selling books. You can write many more if you wish, but never will you have an opportunity like this again."

Intrigued, McMannis took another step downwards, thinking that surely he was mad for following this lunatic and, indeed, that one thought seemed to bring some clarity to the situation. Either I am mad, he thought, or this is all a dream. Yes, of course, that's it. I nodded off in the darkness, in the studio, and that's where I physically am right now, asleep in the chair. With that happy thought, he plunged downwards to the bottom of the stairs.

The dapper gent stood by an old wooden door. His hand grasped its brass handle. "Oh, good," he cried, "you *have* come. I knew you would. But now, before I open this door, there are a few things we need to get out of the way. Would you prefer to call me Satan, Lucifer, Beelzebub or just plain old 'The Devil?'"

Oh, ho, so you're the Devil, McMannis thought. What a lark! Such a wonderful dream! I should have guessed. I should have known. "'The Devil' is fine," he said. He was, in fact, now enjoying himself immensely. Certainly, he'd never had a dream with such lucidity before, but that was the wondrous part about it: safely asleep in his chair and out on an adventure at the very same time.

"Yes, that's the name I prefer too. I like it because it has the word 'evil' in it." The Devil grinned wickedly. "Now, when I open the door, remembered they won't be able to see us. I have taken certain precautions that will allow for complete and clandestine observation. There is a table to the left of the roulette wheel that has been specially reserved for us. We shall move straight to the table and take our seats. Then we shall talk some more."

"Marvellous," McMannis said, "absolutely marvellous."

The Devil opened the door. The buzz of a crowd reached McMannis's ears. The smell of thick tobacco and stale alcohol rose to his nostrils. The Devil took him by the arm and drew him towards the table.

"Have a vodka," the Devil said, as he pushed McMannis's chair in for him.

For a moment, McMannis sat there stunned. He studied the dark thickset men around the roulette table, marvelled at the glorious beards they wore. Certainly, they were not in Brisbane anymore. "Are we in Russia somewhere?" he asked.

"St Petersburg. And there is your great writer, Dostoyevsky. The same man who inspired you," the Devil said, waving his hand dismissively towards the roulette table. "Look at him, the miserly kopek-pinching rouble-squandering wretch, chasing the numbers on that silly wheel night after night. A great gambler he says he will become, but always he loses. It has no effect on him. Does he return to his writing? Does he honour the deal he made with me? No, my dear sir, he does not, so in grip of that silly spinning wheel is he. There are others worse than I, you see, that continue to lend him money. And while he has money, the wheel has him and he will not write. You see my predicament, I trust. The great books must be written, but I have only this inveterate gambler to work through."

McMannis was about to ask about the precise nature of the deal that the Devil had done with Dostoyevsky, but then something else of far greater importance suddenly struck him. "But his books *have* already been written," he said.

"How so?" the Devil asked, an honestly bedazzled expression on his face.

"We'll, because I've read them."

"Yes . . . "

"So how could I read them if they haven't been written?"

"Because you wrote them."

McMannis chuckled, took a sip of his vodka. How absurd this dream was becoming. "Impossible. Ridiculous," he said, but he was enjoying himself well. What a wonderful fantasy his mind had concocted for his entertainment.

"It's why I brought you here. Why I need your assistance. You must understand. Together you and I will write Dostoyevsky's novels for him. Ghost writers if you like. I have the ideas, the same ideas I promised to give to him and you know how to write. Together we will make a fantastic team. I promise to be your greatest muse. I will never desert you. I will be there, just behind your left shoulder as you write. You can live here, right in St Petersburg. I'll find you a lovely little garret, a pleasant one with lots of light and air. You will have enough roubles to live comfortably, but not excessively. And the occasional nice lady, of course, will come round to visit. It will be lots of hard work, but fun too."

"No, no, you are missing my point," McMannis said. "The books *are* written. I can walk into a bookshop or a library in Brisbane, anywhere, and find all those great novels written by Dostoyevsky."

"Only because you are here tonight and will, I trust, in a very short while, agree to assist me. Temporality is circular and folding. It has so many layers moving in and around each other. The future, the past, the present are all wrapped up together. Time is not linear even though it is efficient for humans to believe it is. So if *you* do not write Dostoyevsky's novels, they will not be written."

The Devil clicked his fingers. McMannis suddenly found himself sitting in a shabby poorly lit office, studying a sheath of papers. It was not one of his novels. It was a report that one of his junior engineers had prepared on the specifications for the new tunnel under the Brisbane River. The report was important, but he kept looking at the clock, hoping that it was time to knock off, so he could head to the pub to have a few beers with his mates.

The Devil clicked his fingers again. McMannis looked up from his glass of vodka. "An engineer?" he said.

"But, of course," the Devil said. "You have not agreed to assist me. 'The Brothers Karamazov' was never written. You never read the book that inspired you to write when you were young. It is your future too that hangs in the balance."

McMannis realised that his wonderful dream was suddenly taking on the shades of a very disturbing nightmare. To think that the Devil was telling him he would be the source of his own inspiration. It was diabolical. But then another thought struck him.

"Why is it important for you that Dostoyevsky's books be written? If you really are the Devil, what would you care about what becomes of me or the loss of a few famous books to the world?"

"Oh, just vanity on my part," the Devil said, smiling and flashing a set of splendid white teeth. "I want to be a writer. I have the ideas, but not the skills. But you . . . "

"You're lying," McMannis said.

"How can you tell?" the Devil asked and shifted in his chair.

"You're voice goes all oily and smooth."

"Really? I've never noticed that before," the Devil said.

"Yes, it does," McMannis said. "So what's the deal between you and Dostoyevsky?"

The Devil's eyes narrowed. He spat out the words. He could not help himself. "Look at that miserable scoundrel over there. He sold me his soul in return for being a great writer. And now he has reneged on the bargain. He thinks he has me beaten. You see, he believes his soul is safe, as long as he refuses to write, as long as his books are not written. But they will be written. You and I will write them, but they will be published under his name and he *will* be hailed as a great writer. His soul will be mine. I win. He loses. That's the simple truth of it."

The Devil thumped his fist down on the table, picked up a glass of vodka and drank it down in one go. He smacked his lips, then stuck his thumb on the tip of his nose and wriggled his fingers towards the roulette table.

"No," McMannis said. "I won't be part of this."

"What?" the Devil cried. "I don't believe you. Aren't you tempted? This is your chance to write something great, something wonderful and substantial. The books will be lost. Your inspiration too. Your whole career. Believe me when I tell you that you will be paid handsomely."

"I'm a writer," McMannis said. "So is he. Fyodor Mikhailovich Dostoyevsky. In a moment of weakness, you got him, but now he's beaten you. I'm not going to do anything to help you. It's up to him to decide whether he wants to write or not."

"You're an engineer," the Devil said, clicking his fingers. "There are plenty more writers where you came from."

McMannis looked up at the clock. It was Friday afternoon, time to knock-off and head down to the pub, but instead he got up and closed his office door. He returned to his desk, opened the word processor up and wrote the following words:

At about nine o'clock in the morning at the end of November, when the jacaranda blossoms had begun to fall, the train from Sydney was approaching Brisbane at full speed. It was so bright and sunny, the light reflected so fiercely, that people could barely see anything out of the carriage windows . . .

Bloody awful, McMannis thought, when he read what he'd written, but then he read it again and realised it was not such a bad start.

Around about the same time, in a gambling den in St Petersburg, while the Devil was in despair in his cups—no writers had come to his aid—the roulette wheel spun and the ball rolled, and a young professional gambler by the name of Fyodor Mikhailovich Dostoyevsky pushed the last of his roubles onto a little square that bore the number '24'.

The wheel stopped. The ball spun around and around and around. The Devil wagged a drunken finger at him, but Dostoyevsky was already up and dancing. His number had finally come up. Towers of roubles tumbled towards him. It was vodka on the house. He was kissing everyone in the place. He even went up and gave the Devil a great big lip-smacker on the face, but the Devil was too drunk to notice. Fyodor was the toast of town that night and soon become a gambler of great renown. Later in life, living in a chalet in Switzerland, he would say to his friends, over expensive champagne, "I once wished to be a writer. What a silly naive fool I was then."

A BARGAIN WITH THE WRITER

Michael S. Martin

For Elinor

The devil does not exist, the devil does not exist . . . I kept telling myself this as the handset grew warmer and the room colder.

"Look, who is this? What do you want?" I demanded. I made sure the malice in my voice was unmistakeable. For each of the last three calls there had been nothing but silence at the other end.

"You couldn't possibly live without me," replied the caller finally, "you need me and you know it!"

Not again! The statement stung me. I contemplated that last sentence a moment. Was it true? It was an abhorrent and despicable thought if it was. *The devil does not exist . . .* I was losing my grip a little on the handset; my palms were sweating, my fingers trembling. A curious sweaty chill came upon me—my extremities were the warning sign—there was a chill at my elbow and at the nape of my neck. Unconsciously, I was gathering my shirt collar closer around my neck and I was starting to feel a little threatened.

"Look, who is this?" I demanded again, but knowledge preceded the enquiry. Silence. Of course, the devil does not exist. Was I childishly trying to reassure myself by pretending to question who it was on the other end of the phone? Who was I trying to kid? Again, one stray thought was all it took . . . and then:

"As I told you before, in writing there is only death and love," he said, "and you once again have love, so here I am."

I felt palpitations in my chest. "What do you want?" I asked.

"You called me, remember?" said the devil.

"No," I lied, embarrassed, "you called me." Was I so lost?

"Really?" was the nonchalant reply. The room was becoming noticeably colder, chilly even, and the blank screen of my computer was dimming. "I only answer when called upon. You know that death only comes to those who wish to receive it."

I was aware that the handset was becoming very cold as it slipped some more in my sweaty grasp. I gathered my courage; I'd been here before. "You can't confound me with your trickery. My faith in love has overcome you," I said.

"Ah, you do remember me . . . at last. Your wife, so sad," he said. "So, your new love, she's, ah, well I hope . . . "? He trailed off.

I felt sick in my guts. "Yes, I've found love again, in spite of you!" I said.

"In *spite* of me? Hmm, love. What is that, some kind of shield? Something you protect yourself with? Do you think you can protect yourself with love, your loved ones? Where is this shield each time I come to take your precious loved ones?" asked the devil.

My heart sank.

"Love! What a thing to trade!" he needled.

I was taken aback somewhat. My eyes came to rest on the two gold-framed photos on my desk. "You may present yourself as the antithesis of love but you are merely a persuasive distraction," I said. "No one *wishes* to receive death. Death has always simply been a part of life. It's a contract. There is no life without death. Love is our way of overcoming death." The handset warmed a little and I began to relax. Am I such a hypocrite, I wondered.

"Then why did you call?" asked the devil.

The handset went cold again.

"It didn't seem to work the last time now, did it?" he sneered.

"Look, I don't need you!" I said insistently. What a liar I was!

"Very well." There was a sharp click as the phone went dead.

I wanted to put the handset back in its cradle, but I found that I could not uncurl my fingers from it. It was now so cold it had very quickly become frosty as the sweat from my palm and fingers had turned to ice. I shivered. Was it from the cold or that curious desire that compelled me again? There, I admitted it . . .

Once again the words had stopped flowing. The computer screen was inanimate for the foreseeable future. Was I losing my grip on love? Was I destined to betray? Confusion rose in me. In frustration, I rose from my chair. "Is that what you want," I yelled into the phone, "for me to stop writing about you, telling people what you're really like? Do you think you can intimidate me? I'm not a plaything. You can't toy with me."

No answer.

I sat down again, breathing heavily. I tried to gather my thoughts. What if I simply refused to believe in death, just put the phone down? Forget the whole thing, walk away from it all. What need is there for death when love is all there is? Of course, we die physically, I thought, but we are not prey to death. We transcend death through memory and love and writing. Death is *our* prey. Everyday we inch our way towards conquering it, but still—and here's the rub—we console ourselves with the hope that those who read us and love us will eternally remember us when we do pass. Could I do something else, instead of writing? Could I go back to teaching, persuade the young to take up the cause . . . ?

There was another click as the phone came alive again. He was back.

"Oh, no," the devil said, "if I wanted you to stop writing about me especially, I would simply leave you be. Eventually the words would stop . . . again."

I said nothing. He was right. I knew it.

"Conquer death, will you?" he sneered. "How many more will you make suffer? Tell her. Tell her right now. Go on. Go up and wake her and tell her the bargain we're about to make. No one can read your words if there are none . . . ."

"What bargain?" I hissed.

"Oh, please," he laughed, "you had no trouble writing again after I took the last one, did you?"

It was true. To console myself, I shut out all others for a long time and healed myself with words.

"Love would not exist if it were not for death," he said. "What need would you have for love were it not for me? Your contentment is what stops you from writing. What if I took this one too, hmm? You would have more words than you could write."

I felt the blood draining from my face.

"You are frail and weak. When my darkness comes, you reach out to another for comfort and reassurance. To feel their touch, their warmth, as my cold devours you. Am I not more than a persuasive distraction?"

"We *will* conquer death," I insisted. "The scientists say my children might be the last generation to die or may even be the first to live forever. Then what? For you, I mean?"

"And they still require this love?" he asked.

"Of course, it's our basic instinct," I said.

"No," he countered, "that's just rat lust. What comfort or succour will you require, if you are content that you will live forever, if you did not anticipate death, if there is no uncertainty in life? This love you talk of is *just* a persuasive distraction, an artefact of desire, a mere sexual release on occasion, surely?"

I was nervous and fearful. "I don't mean sex alone. I mean real love, you fool, sexual union, the completeness hungered for by all of us, to allow two to become one—and it can only come through our love, otherwise all you're having is sex." I felt my grip on the handset thawing.

"What's wrong with just having sex?" he asked. "I can arrange all the sex you want, the best you'll ever have. I'm very good at arranging such things, you know. I've tempted the very best of you, in fact. I was called by one of your greatest in the desert once and I very nearly . . . ."

"You're not listening," I said angrily. "I'm talking of the real love that reveals us, you bastard. What would you know of love anyway?"

There was a sudden shot of pain down my arm as ice made my grip solid once more.

"Be very careful; I am close by," he rasped in a low voice. "Would you be prepared to die for this love? I can swiftly arrange that too. Shall we put you to the test . . . here . . . .now? You never know, she might take up the writing from where you'll leave off . . . "

I had a moment of panic. I felt that awe-filling sickly experience of terror and dread.

"Well?" he asked.

I was boiling in turmoil. I had failed the most basic test. After spruiking love, my first instinct was to escape the test of it.

"No, I thought not. As I said, you are frail and weak."

Was I? Was that the truth of it? Perhaps, but failure can also be a strength! That is the reason we reach out to one another in difficult times, not for succour, but for forgiveness and strength. Strength to suffer death. There is no meaning in frivolously throwing one's life away, which is all accepting the devil's test would succeed in doing. True to form, shallow not deep. The true test of love is strength, forgiveness and courage and that test has to be witnessed and be instructive so that the truth of love could be revealed to others.

"So, are you willing to test this love of yours?" he said.

"Yes," I stammered, "as long as you are prepared to live. There! That's *my* bargain. Talk's cheap. Show me that you are prepared to take life knowing what I know, feeling what I have felt, loving as I have been loved. In return, I accept death, knowing all I do about *you*"

The line went dead again. Warmth returned to my hand and the icy pain began to recede.

I took a long time to put the phone back on its hook that night. I still had no words, but they would come, I hoped. Some time later, I turned my back on the cold, left the room and headed upstairs to curl up in bed with the warmth of the one that loved me, that I loved. The next morning I told her everything. That same afternoon she was killed in a car accident.

ICE CUBE

Chris McMahon

"Hey, I'm down here."

My heart skipped a beat, and I looked into the exposed ice-cubes of my glass in surprise.

Shining ghostly across the jagged planes of a fractured ice-cube was a man with a trident-beard and a high widow's peak.

"Flashbacks to Dr Who," I murmured, thinking he looked just like the Master, the Doctor's famous adversary.

The face creased in impatience.

I shook my head, but the image remained.

I lifted the bottle of bourbon and tipped it gently, trying to drown the ice-cubes. The summer sun was delicious on my skin as I leant over the garden-lounge and placed the bottle carefully on my lawn. I was not going to waste a drop. Not today.

I lay back and sighed, staring morosely into the green subtropical tangle of my backyard where a huge macadamia nut tree now towered over gnarled old mango trees and my once domesticated philodendrons, grown wild and huge, raced up their trunks.

"I'm not going away," he said, his tiny yet authoritative voice undiminished by the layers of amber spirit I had poured on top of him.

Six hours ago, I got the call from Go Books. I can still hear the voice of the commissioning editor as she delivered the news. My fourth book—the vessel of my hope and dreams—was rejected. "But we would like to see more of your work, of course. The sales department thought it just outside the list. Cross-genre, you know, very hard to market."

"Now what?" I said to the little man in the glass.

"You know who I am?" he asked, his face imperious.

"No, and I don't care," I said, taking another belt of bourbon from the glass and adding more before he had a chance to speak.

"Listen!" he said. "I'm the d . . ."

"I don't care," I said, cutting him off. "I don't care about anything, anymore."

"Really?" he said, smiling.

Where was Dr Who when you needed him?

"What if I could give you a killer plot? One that Go Books would sign up for in a shot? With a guaranteed hook? A sure-fire setting that would stick you right in the middle of the marketing girls' target lists?"

I had received ideas from strange places before, but a talking ice-cube was the weirdest yet.

But could I handle it again? Another wasted year for a doorstop rejected by every publisher on the planet? How did I know if I could trust this ice-cube guy?

"Ah, but not this one," he said. "This one will go straight to the commissioning editor and race through acquisitions faster than Harry Potter on steroids. And you can trust me, I assure you of that."

"Hey, did you just read my mind?"

"Of course, I can read your mind. I'm the d . . ."

"Ah!" I interrupted. "A delusion already has the inside track. I've got you there."

I refilled the glass.

"Well, how about it?" he said.

My head was humming, and I noted with some apprehension that the bottle was almost finished. What the heck, I thought, pouring the last of the bourbon into my glass; it's not every day that you miss your seventeenth close call at success after twelve years of hard work, hopes and dreams.

"Well?" he prompted.

I stared at his little face, hoping he would go away. No such luck.

"Okay," I said. "What if you could?" My determination to bury my dreams, once and for all, shattered. Beneath was the desperate desire to write, to express—to soar. To start again.

Am I insane? Why do I do this to myself?

"Oh, I can," he said, his eyes glittering cruelly. "I mean, what are you going to do? Re-write it *again*? Go to another Masterclass? Take a risk on another inspiration? I can give you a winner."

"Yeah? Well, what's the catch?" I said.

"There is no such thing as a free lunch," he said, chuckling. "A little phrase I picked up from my days selling insurance."

I glared at the ice-cube, refusing to be baited. If he was on the sell, let him sell.

His smile became a grimace.

"The catch is I give you every story from here on in. No more midnight inspirations. No more startling originals. You write the stories I tell you to write."

"But . . ."

"Oh, don't worry," he said. "I can guarantee you that they will sell *very* well—adjusted to the times, supremely marketable. Nothing too daring, but tight and entertaining nonetheless."

"Every story?" I said.

"But think of the money," he said. "The fame, the *women*! Remember that three million dollar house on the river? The one you fantasised about? It could be yours by this time next year, with an income to match."

"But the ideas . . . it's why I started writing in the first place."

"Ideas," he spat. "Dime a dozen. Why do you think there are so many failed writers? The market doesn't want anything new. Come on, what do you really want?"

The empty bottle of Bourbon slipped from my fingers to thud into the lawn. I squeezed my eyes shut. "No," I said. "I can't let those ideas die."

"Another damn writer whinging about his ideas!" he said, then sighed. "I was offering it to you on a platter."

I opened my eyes and looked down at him. He seemed puzzled.

"I don't understand what's wrong with you writers. I never have the same trouble with lawyers. They're just ideas, you know. Sure you won't change your mind?"

I shook my head, not trusting myself to speak.

"Okay, I'll try the Brisbane Writers' festival. It worked well for me last year."

He disappeared with a tiny pop, and I sat, staring as the ice-cube slowly melted.

"Damn," I said. "What the Hell *am* I going to write next?"

TIME TO WRITE

Jason Nahrung

Jim Brown walked, head down, finger playing absently with the hole in his jeans pocket. He hardly noticed the people on the sidewalk, damn near walked through a red signal onto the road. He almost had it figured. The good old murder in the locked room scenario. All he was missing was how the killer got out . . .

Weariness from his tedious day at the store weighed him down, making his shoulders sag and his mind grow foggy, as though he had been injected with anaesthetic. If only he had more time to work on his book, to come at it fresh. But work and friends just wouldn't give him a break. And it wasn't like he could just closet himself away all the time. He had to have some social life.

Ha! Friday night. The street was damp from a twilight shower that had left the air crisp and clear and full of promise, and all he had to look forward to was a leftover pizza in the microwave and a video before bed, and then another shift at the store. If he could just figure out this last element of his story, he knew the rest of it would flow. He'd be back in the zone. Back on track . . . if he could just find the time to write it down.

And then he bumped into someone.

He staggered back, annoyed at his own clumsiness, and just a little pissed the person hadn't got the hell out of his way. Couldn't they see he was *thinking*?

He looked up and his annoyance fled.

"Sorry," he stammered.

The girl smiled.

"My fault," she said, and caressed his arm apologetically. He felt heat through his t-shirt sleeve where her fingers—long and thin, with perfect, unpainted nails—touched. Her voice was husky, like she'd spent too many hours shouting to be heard in a smoke-filled club. Her eyes were glittering green, set in a pale face with a frame of crimson hair. Her body was to die for. Oh, man . . . if only.

Jim went to walk around her.

Her hand tightened on his upper arm. "Isn't that Michael Towers in there?"

"What?" He froze, as much due to her words as her grip.

Awareness dawned. He was outside Dymocks, at the edge of a foot-path-blocking throng spilling out through the doors, their overcoats and cardigans all but obscuring the sign: *Michael Towers, book signing*.

Jim gritted his teeth and looked over the assembled heads in the direction the girl pointed.

"Yeah, that's him," he said. They'd put Towers on a dais, the better to lord over his subjects as they grovelled before him, books held out expectantly waiting for his biro blessing.

"That's his third best seller, isn't it?" the girl asked.

"Yeah, something like that."

"Do you know him? I mean, he's from Brisbane, isn't he?"

Jim hunched his shoulders and looked to the street as a taxi splashed by. Bile ate at his gut. "Yeah, he's a local. We were in the same writing class at uni."

"Oh really?" The girl seemed very excited, moved closer to him. She was about his height. He felt her breast push against his bare arm, her leg against his. Wasn't she cold after the rain? Just wearing that skirt, that top? Not a sign of goose pimples he could see, but then, the light wasn't that great out here in the street.

"So what do you think of him? Do you like his books?" the girl asked, and her breath smelt of cherries, or maybe strawberries. God, her eyes were unbelievably green. Jim blinked.

"Everything okay?" she asked, leaning back.

"Yeah, sure," Jim said, and stared at her eyes again. Just for a moment there, he'd thought the pupils had slitted, vertically, like a cat's. But no, her eyes were normal; gorgeous, but normal.

"So?" she said, smiling again.

"Huh?"

"What do you think of Towers?"

"Oh, him? He's an arsehole."

The girl flinched and Jim regretted his venom.

"I mean," he said, hurrying, aware the girl was still holding his arm, "he's had lucky breaks, that's all. I didn't know him that well, really."

Well enough, though, Jim thought. Towers had been a straight 'A' student, and popular too. He had the best laptop on the market, the fancy car, the pretty girls chasing him. His parents had even bought him a unit near the uni; no share housing and after-hours, minimum-wage welcome-to-your-HECS-debt job for Mr Towers.

"I suppose that happens," the girl said, waving both hands in a conciliatory way. The action made Jim aware that her breasts moved freely beneath her top, but had all the poise of a fully underwired set. His mouth went dry as he tried to work out why she was still talking to him.

"So, you're a writer too?" she asked, eyes wide with interest. Her lips appeared to be untouched by makeup, but were glossy and full.

"Yeah, I am," Jim said, surprising himself with his fervour.

"What have you written?" she asked, and his sudden confidence sank way past the clutches of his hands, once more balled firmly in his pockets.

"Nothing you would have read," he mumbled, and left it at that. A bit hard to read something that hasn't even been finished, let alone submitted.

"Oh? I love reading," she said. "I love writers." She licked her lips, teeth so white, tongue so pink. "My name's Lucy." She held out a hand.

He shook it reluctantly, feeling clumsy and just a bit false.

"Jim," he said. "Jim Brown." Such a dull name; he'd be using a pseudonym when he got published, maybe something starting with an F, so he could be close to Freddie Forsyth. Any letter but T.

"So what do you write?" Lucy asked.

He shrugged his shoulders, aware of a numbing heat running up his hand where hers still gripped it.

"Whatever takes my fancy."

"Really?" A perfect eyebrow arched and, as though released from some secret gland, a waft of subtly sweet perfume washed over him. "Sounds interesting. Do you have time to tell me about it?"

"Time?" he said, and removed his hand from hers to run it through his hair, moderately surprised it still held movement. The numbness had reached his chest; he felt short of breath, a little light-headed. "I wish."

Her eyebrow lowered, her lips pouted, her eyes clouded.

"Oh, what the hell," he gushed. "It can wait. Um, where do you wanna go?" He eyed the bookstore warily. The crowd had edged further indoors, closer to their prophet.

"How about my place?" she said, and took his arm in hers.

"Didn't you want to get a book signed?" Jim asked, willing his feet to get back on the concrete. What the hell was happening here?

"Can you keep a secret?"

"Um, sure."

"I'm not a big fan of Mr Towers." He glimpsed a flash of anger in those green eyes, like a cat that had just let the fattest, dumbest pigeon slip through its claws. She leaned closer, those emerald orbs fixed on him, and he wondered if the pigeon would feel like this: scared and expectant, both at the same time. "I was actually his first agent, but he dumped me, went to the opposition. They even got him out of his contract with me, cited some loophole or other."

Jim felt her nails digging into his arm. Her teeth seemed very sharp.

"I knew he was an arsehole," Jim said, and managed to wrest himself free of both her gaze and her claws before any harm was done.

Lucy nodded, then her features softened into a giggle and a playful pat against his chest.

"C'mon," she said, "you can tell me about your writing while we walk. My apartment isn't far, just down by the river."

The Brisbane River looked different from thirty stories up, glittering with the lights of boats and reflections from the highrises lining its banks. The inky water occasionally rippled in the wake of a passing CityCat ferry, making the lights dance.

Jim stood at the window of Lucy's bedroom, daringly showing his naked form to anyone who could see through the tinted glass. Ice in a glass of bourbon tinkled in his hand. He smelt of sex, furious, joyous, wonderful sex.

He heard the satin sheets slither and then smelt Lucy, felt her as she wrapped herself around him.

"Nice view," she said.

"It looks beautiful from up here," he said, pointing with his glass as cars streamed under the pointed arches of the Story Bridge.

"I was talking about your arse," she said, and slapped him. He jumped, spilled his drink, turned to face her. She had pulled a sheet around her but it had slipped to her waist.

"That's a cute tat," he said, reaching towards her left breast.

"Excuse me?" she said in mock outrage, intercepting his hand.

"I said *tat*."

"Oh," she said with a cheeky smile, and let his fingers find the ink. "My little devil."

He'd hardly noticed it before, but then, only the bedside light had been on, and they'd been busy . . . The tattoo felt warm, warmer than her skin, the red, horned face beaming out from the side of one firm breast.

"Cute," he said.

She took his hand and led him back to the bed, so that they lay side by side, propped up on pillows. She lit a cigarette, offered it to him but he declined. Couldn't afford to smoke.

She exhaled a noxious cloud and said, "So, all you need is time."

"Eh?"

"Time to write. You were saying the reason Towers made it so big was because he doesn't actually have to work. He has all the time in the world just to write. And you don't."

"That's about it. I'm just so tired after work, y'know . . . "

"I understand. What if I told you, I knew a way you could have all the time in the world?"

"What? How?" Lucy was clearly well-heeled. Was she proposing to keep him while he wrote? *My god* . . . He looked around the room, so simply yet expensively decorated. He must've been good . . . Actually, he could feel the itch of scratches in his back that suggested just how good he'd been. Jim held the glass in both hands, afraid of his sudden shaking spilling bourbon on the bed.

"It wouldn't be *that* easy," she said, ruminating over her cigarette. "But I did it for Towers. I could do it for you too."

Bourbon splashed over the rim of Jim's glass. Even his voice shook. "God, Lucy, I'd do anything. You give me the time, and you won't be disappointed. And I would never shaft you like that arsehole did."

She leaned down, pink tongue lapping the spilt bourbon from his hand, teeth nipping at the soft flesh near his thumb.

"I think we have a deal, Mr Brown," she growled. "Drink up, you've got some work to do."

Jim sits in his cell, picking at the keys of his typewriter. He'd have preferred a computer, but the old Olivetti was all he could muster for now.

He sighs, staring at the graffiti on the wall, looking for the words.

"She fucked me, but good," he types, reads it, then rips the paper out and scrunches it up. He swears and retrieves it, smoothes it out, and tries to feed it back through the rollers. He can't afford to waste paper.

He taps the keys again, grimacing as he works the carriage return and jams the uneven paper.

Fifteen years they'd given him for killing Towers. All the time in the world to write. Now, how to get the murderer out of the locked room?

SHARP

Richard Pitchforth

The worst thing about the Devil is that he is absolutely honest.

At first I didn't notice him. When I did I named him Sharp, because at the time I had no idea who he really was. Labelling strangers is a game I play in my head, and Sharp just seemed to fit. He emanated a gambler's wariness, and had an aura of danger about him; an amalgam of sensuous speed, and the way he noted everything without moving his head.

I should have been editing my book, an opus five years in gestation. Instead I spent the morning deciding whether to return the first three chapters of a lightweight romantic thriller my ex-girlfriend, Debbie, had given me to critique. I hadn't written a single comment, the result (I told myself) of vengefulness, rather than my usual laziness. Returning the pages unmarked would be more than a gesture—it would display my complete indifference.

In the end, I decided that I couldn't deal with seeing Debbie. I tossed the chapters back on my desk and went out.

So, I was not supposed to be at the Regatta at 11.30 a.m. on a weekday morning, but it seemed the best option after wasting the morning thinking about Debbie. The pub looks like a Mississippi river boat aground on the river bank. Triple J said the temperature was over twenty-seven degrees C, and the humidity meant any movement was like exercising in a sweat lodge. I sat at a table and closed my eyes, breathing in the mixed scents of jasmine and hops before I sipped the froth from an ice-cold schooner of beer.

From the veranda, I looked across Coronation Drive, watching yellow buses plough through carpets of purple flowers under moulting jacaranda trees. Beyond this, the Brisbane River carried a constant parade of blue ferries and scarlet rowers, and the occasional wanker on a jet ski. On the far banks, yellow wattles and crimson bougain-villea were interspersed between green and violet plants. Queensland celebrates spring with the verve of Bollywood.

I had thought all the tables were empty, awaiting the midday rush of chattering university students and women who lunch, but then I became aware somebody occupied the table next to me. I hadn't seen him sit down.

Sharp gently flicked open a copy of the *Courier Mail* as he sipped a coke and something. It was probably bourbon. He looked like a bourbon sort of guy. Ice rattled in the glass when he put it down. He wore boat shoes and an open neck shirt. His eyes were hidden by black sunglasses, and he might have been thirty, or fifty. Somehow I just couldn't put a finger on his age. I felt his gaze from behind his shades and looked away, obeying a personal code that says you respect a punter's privacy while he picks a winner at Doomben. Betting in Bris-bane is a different kind of gamble—you have to guess what races the insiders are fixing, not which horse is fastest. The corner of Sharp's mouth turned up.

"You bet sometimes?" he asked in an educated local accent.

I shook my head. "Writers have no money to waste, except on beer." Or women, I thought bitterly.

"Fair enough," he said, then added, "I know a lot of writers."

Two huge crows settled noisily on the handrail of the wrought iron balustrade behind him. He turned to smile at them, the way some people regard a neighbour's small pet dog.

I drank my beer, seeing him as a distorted black shape through the bottom of my glass. Blokes who drink before midday have darker corners than most, but I was not one of them. Not really. I just needed a little anaesthetising since Debbie left: two weeks and three days ago. I fought the temptation to work out the additional hours. My foolishness had cost me dearly, but I consoled myself with the thought I was surviving. We tell ourselves lies to keep us sane.

When I looked back I found a woman had joined Sharp. Her skin was luminous, and she wore a fashionable blue hat that accentuated her high cheekbones and shaded her eyes. Her long, bare, smooth legs vanished beneath her short silk dress, suggesting mysteries I was keen to learn more about. I filled with a throbbing heat. My blood ran thick and slow in my veins. I watched her red nails tap the side of her sunglasses with a slim finger and it felt as if we had met before, as if we had shared some secret in a past life. Her wry grin seemed to mock me. My hand shook as I drained my glass. I tried to look everywhere but at her.

"Let me get you another," Sharp said. I was surprised he included me in the shout, and more so when I saw the barman arrive the moment he finished speaking, fresh drinks already set up on his silver tray. I didn't have to time to decline. The barman was already returning to the bar with a yellow fifty dollar note, and a smile from the young woman that made him walk into the edge of the door.

Sharp raised his glass. "To originality," he said, cocking his head quizzically and looking at me until I responded. The young woman touched her glass to his, then leaned over to clink her glass with mine. I only had time for a mouthful, but Sharp's glass was already empty. He stood in one fluid movement, and tucked his paper under his arm.

"See you later," he said to the young woman, touching her lightly on the cheek as he left. Then he turned to me and said, "Enjoy yourself." He smiled, and I watched as he left the sunny veranda and stepped into the gloom of the hotel's interior. When I turned to speak to the young woman, I found she had moved her chair to my table.

"Shouldn't you go with him?" I asked.

She shook her head and leaned back, amused. "No, I think I'll stay. I find you interesting."

"Doesn't he get jealous?"

She looked amused again. "Him? Why should he? He never feels envy. Or jealousy."

"He's lying." I could not imagine any man not feeling possessive of her.

"Oh, no." She leaned forward, and I could not help peering down her cleavage at the soft swell of her breasts. I could have sworn her nipples hardened as I watched. "I know him. He never, ever lies."

She leaned back and caught my eye, making it clear she knew exactly what I had been doing. She gave a little laugh at my discomfort. "He's the most ethical person ever. People just don't measure up to his standards. It's a source of constant disappointment to him."

That should have warned me, but my brain had switched off. I watched the fall of her hair, the tilt of her throat. I gave up listening for anything other than hints she was available, and willing to satisfy the mixture of curiosity, lust, and bravado that fuels a man aroused by such a woman.

We may have stayed at the pub the whole afternoon, or perhaps it was less than ten minutes. I never could reconstruct the rest of that day. I remember she smelled of crushed flowers and lemons and limes as she writhed naked beneath me in my bed. Recollection says the taste of her was smoother than ice-cream, and her skin slid over mine like warm oil. My memory can play in slow motion the way her closed eyes fluttered, and the flash of white teeth as she bit her lower lip with pleasure. She stayed with me for hours of blissful coupling, until she surged with me towards release and a series of shuddering pinnacles that swept us out to distant shores and then brought us thundering back to breathless exhaustion in a cycle that seemed never-ending. Her perfection beside me was the only image I wanted to hold in my mind forever.

Afterwards, as I held her gently and drifted off to sleep, I heard mynah birds hold their sunset squabbles outside my window, heard thunder in the distant clouds, wind rustling in the palms, and wattle seeds rattling across my tin roof.

She slipped away as I slept.

When I awoke, I still remembered what Debbie had done to me, but now it was like watching someone else's grief. Instead I wanted the nameless woman. The need for her was like acid, eating through my flesh and burning up my soul. I had never before truly desired anything. It was not enough to tangle tongues and press together our sweaty bellies, not enough to pull her body hard against me as desire roared in my ears and dominated my whole being. There were deep, dangerous currents between us; viscous thoughts rooted in heat and lust. I longed to penetrate her every pore, to share our fluids. Teasing thoughts of debauchery swept through my mind. Hot pounding lust seized my loins and left my hands shaking and my breath quickening, before I even lifted the corner of my fantasies.

I returned to the Regatta the next day, expecting, after what had happened between us, she would be there waiting for me. But there was no sign of her, and no sign of Sharp either. I stayed at the pub all day, drinking slowly, prowling the bars and verandas, telling myself either one of them would turn up at any minute. But they didn't, not that day, nor the one after.

For the next week or so I staked out the Regatta. I'd arrive early in the morning and leave late at night when the last drunks piled into their taxi cabs. On my way, I'd drop into the local TABs, just in case Sharp might be there, laying down a bet. Once or twice I even went out to the city's twin racetracks, thinking they might be places Sharp liked to hang out.

After that, I took to wandering the city aimlessly, day and night, checking everywhere — discos and libraries, trendy cafes and tired warehouses; anywhere there was even a small chance I might run into them.

When I gave up, I returned to my computer, soul sick but resigned to writing.

"Where the hell have you been?" Hartley said on the phone. Hartley was my last remaining friend and maybe editor, good-natured and perennially puzzled by my laziness.

"I've been ill," I said, and realised it was apposite. I looked out the window. A two-foot long lizard baked in the late afternoon sun. I told Hartley I was no closer to having the manuscript ready for him to look at.

"You have a lot to catch up on, mate. Get on with it," he said.

After I hung up, I pulled the bloody manuscript towards me. Even as I looked at it, I imagined the mystery woman reclining on the white paper as if it were a bedsheet, sweat forming fine drops between her breasts. Her body undulated with sexual invitation; siren songs echoed just beyond my hearing. My hands started to shake. I picked up a pen, but it fell from my fingers. The hell with the book!

I returned to the Regatta once more.

"Trouble?"

I looked up from my table. It was Sharp, he who had been untraceable.

"Where is she?"

"I don't know."

I'm not a physical man, but I rose from my chair and gripped his elegant lapels. We stood so close our shirt buttons almost tangled, then I breathed out slowly and let go. "You're lying," I said.

He looked at me calmly, and it felt as if layers of my brain were peeling away. "Actually, I never lie." He shook his head and smiled, and then he said something odd. "Bad press notwithstanding."

"How do I find her?"

"Ah, that's a different matter." He put a hand on my shoulder, and guided me away from the after-work crowd and onto the sidewalk outside. A group stood up from an umbrella-shaded table, and we took their place. I could see several fascinated women and a well-dressed man inside the pub looking out, watching Sharp through the glass. I suppose he was handsome, in a saturnine way.

"I want to talk about this," he said, as he settled into the hardwood chair. He was holding a sheaf of paper: Debbie's first few chapters. Her name was not on the manuscript.

"Where did you get those?" I asked.

Sharp shrugged. "I have ways of getting what I want".

"Your friend took them from my desk?"

Sharp ignored the question. "I like this work of yours. I will publish it. If you give me the rest."

"But . . . "

"You have the rest of it?'

'It's on my computer." At least that was true.

"Come. You're a writer. I'm a publisher. You want to be published, and I can do that."

"I thought you were a gambler," I said.

Sharp tapped the manuscript. "I gamble on lots of things," he said. Then he named an advance that left me tingling and dizzy. "Is it a deal?"

With that much money I could do anything. Take another five years to finish my own book; give the mystery woman whatever she wanted, and again feel her play my body like an angel plays a harp. I segued from greed to lust. "What's her name? Can you find her?"

"I'm sure I could do something. If I wanted to. Give me a reason to want to. Give me the rest of your manuscript."

Debbie's manuscript. Her stupid romantic drivel that had not been invested with a fraction of the work and revision and research I had invested in my book. How could it be worth such a big advance?

It deserved unending rejection, the same way she had rejected me. If she missed out on the big advance it would serve her right. I should accept his offer, not so I could get the money, but to teach Debbie a lesson. You don't dump me without a cost. She might never know, but I would.

Sharp watched me, a small smile playing on his lips, his eyes hidden by his sunglasses. "She is a delightful creature, don't you think? And so comfortable with men who are a financial success." He knew how I needed the woman.

So much money. All I had to do was print off the rest of Debbie's soppy book, maybe change the title, think up an appropriate pseudonym, and give it to Sharp.

But what about Debbie? Could she prove the story was hers? Things might get nasty if she could.

Sharp could tell I was vacillating. "I'll help her find you if you like," he said. I overlooked the odd phrase, but I knew he was taunting me. Pulling me where I should not go.

I was desperate to do something, anything, rather than listen to him any more. I should leave. Drive home. I pulled out my car keys, the ones with the ridiculous spiky metal key ring. It was a gift from Debbie, a gift I no longer wanted because the last thing I needed was a reminder of her. It made me feel sick. I fumbled, trying to pull the keys off the key ring, and a spike jabbed my finger. I put it in my mouth and tasted copper blood. Could I pretend Debbie's book was mine? Could I get away with it? Did I want to? I pushed myself up from the table.

I heard Sharp say, "I'll be here," as I pushed through the crowd towards the car park. Around me, youths in pinstripe suits brayed over Mexican beers, and young professional women swivelled on barstools like cannon on a tank turret, looking for targets. The sun bled from the sky over the hot heart of the city.

Anger and frustration beat at the back of my skull as I stumbled to the car. Frogs roared a chorus from the river and creeks. I sat in the driver's seat, sweat on my forehead and the wheel in my hands, not sure where to go or what to do. All that money. I would have no trouble selling a second book, if the first was as commercially successful as Sharp seemed to believe. But what about Debbie?

I looked up at the Regatta's crowded balcony, hearing the driving music and the shrieks of laughter, saw the clouds of cigarette smoke, and felt myself leap the handrails that bound the path I walked each day.

I decided.

I drove home and returned to give Sharp the manuscript and sign the contract. "Is this your first major sale?" he asked, and I nodded. He looked at me a long time. A strange look. "Have a drink with me to celebrate."

I considered declining, but then I thought the woman might reappear. I didn't want to be with myself. Not that day.

Soon I found I had drunk too much. I remembered when my worst problem was that I just wanted to see the woman. Now everything was worse. So much worse.

Damn Debbie.

Sharp waved his hand, and suddenly she was there, the mystery woman, only a few people away. I stood up from our table, but she looked away, and I saw her smiling across the room. I turned to see what she was looking at.

There was a mirror on the far wall. Beside my reflection was Sharp, now incandescent and awful. I tried to look away, but then I saw the other reflection—the succubus. Its hide was red and green, and as warted as a cane toad's; its mouths leered and suckers waved, and I realised this was the creature I had shared my juices and dreams with on that lust-blasted afternoon.

"Look," Sharp said, and I knew the other person he pointed to in the mirror. Really knew him. It was a reflection I had not dreamed in my worst nightmare, but he showed me the truth. It was me as I had always looked to him: an empty outline of a man with nothing but blackness inside.

"There is not even a tiny hope in there," he hissed. And I began the everlasting despair, because I knew the bastard never lies.

DEVIL VERSUS WRITER

Bronwyn Price

"So, my dear, who exactly do you think you are that you feel you have something of worth to share with the world? Why is it, exactly, that you would so willingly impose your experience on other people?" the Devil inquired.

Well, he had me there. Maybe I didn't have anything worthwhile to say. Maybe my erratic jottings over the years were just unsatisfactorily rehashed garblings of stories told again and again—not adding anything new or of worth to the global psyche.

He was waiting for an answer, but I had none. These conversations with him were becoming less and less comfortable. He shifted his tail and appraised his fingernails.

"Hmmm?" he continued. "What kind of audacity or egotism does a person have to possess to think that their particular view of the world is of any interest to anyone else?" he taunted.

"Egotism?" I ventured. I never thought I *had* an ego to speak of. I write because I need to somehow relieve my overactive brain by spewing words all over a computer screen or whatever piece of paper is at hand at any given moment. "I write because I need to, Devil, don't you see? I thought you understood?" I pleaded. "I've never imposed my writing on anyone. In fact, I think I would rather die than let anyone read anything that I've ever written! You know this."

I was flustered—nervous. Why was he challenging me like this? He usually indulged me in my fantasies. He had become a faithful companion, lulling me into a sense of propriety about my procrastination and multitude of unformed ideas. That's why I kept him around. A little while before we were chatting contentedly over a glass of port and Belgian chocolates . Why was he upping the ante now?

"So, are you trying to tell me that there is not one small part of you that yearns for your words, your particular perspective of the universe, to be shared with the world—and not just shared, but praised and entered into the emotional and psychological reference points of every human being on earth?" he said, turning slightly redder than usual.

"Well . . . " I hesitated. Did he really have to push me like this?

"Are you honestly trying to tell me you have no morsel of an ego that needs to assert its opinion onto paper and, by doing so, make it a permanent entry in the history of recorded thought?" he demanded, nostrils flaring.

"I, ah," I stammered, "I suppose I must confess to a certain desire to be . . . incredibly famous, deferred to for my original take on all things, to be popular and to go down in the annals of literary history." I was like a child being forced to confess to an embarrassing misdeed.

"Ha! See, there we have it. You're all the same, you writers—opinionated egotists who think they can all leave an indelible mark on the world! You know, you really offer me no surprises," he said, bored.

"But surely, Devil, the truly great writers and thinkers and artists of history *have* made an impact on the world. There *is* a place for art and for thought in humanity—how else can people have an anonymous figure in their life offer them empathy—give them comfort and solace that they're not the only ones who think and feel the way they do about existence?"

"Ah—precisely! That's what I loathe about you all—you offer too much courage to the little sheep out there who would otherwise follow me blindly!"

And there I began to realise, from the words of the Devil himself, that art *is* a powerful force, that the expression of ideas for public digestion does indeed have a purpose. That maybe *I* had a purpose. My life.

The Devil saw he was losing my attention. "You know what your problem is, my dear? Your ego, albeit there, is too small, and your fear is too big. I know what you want—you want to be a recognised writer—and you know as well as I do that you can't do it without my help."

He paused, and we eyed each other off in the moment pending the Devil's proposition.

"So here is my solution to this conundrum, my dear. I'll replace your fear with enough of an ego to make you the most infamous writer the world has ever seen," he boasted, smoothing the quiff of hair between his horns.

The devil was offering me the answer to my hidden prayers—except there was just one little hitch. "Devil, you used the word 'infamous', not 'famous', or 'esteemed' or 'respected'—what am I supposed to make of that?"

'Ha! You quibble over my choice of word?'

"Well . . . I *am* a writer . . . I'm wont to quibble over words!"

"Confounded writers!" But regaining his patience, he said, "What I mean, my dear, is that if I do indeed grant you a large ego, I want you to indulge people in their basest instincts, their dark sides, their less noble urges—in a nutshell, you'll be working for me."

"You mean, write something blatantly shocking—just for the sake of it—shock factor literature. No uplifting or unifying messages?"

"None."

Hmmm—I was perplexed. "What if I said no?" I proffered.

"Then you'll be doomed to suffer under your natural ability to observe the world, play with words and write things down, enduring the torture of the uncertainty as to the worthiness of your thoughts—for ever more. It's your choice, my dear."

At this I pondered my future. Infamy or mediocrity? What would it be?

The devil sat and perused me—watching the cogs turn in my head, scrutinising my reaction to the crossroads he'd expertly brought me to. He leaned back in his chair and breathed a long sigh of satisfaction through his nostrils—basking in assumed victory.

I played with the residue of port left in my glass, rolling it around and around, darting rabbit-like glances at my friend, who did not break his gaze and did not break the silence.

I wanted to take his counsel like I had done in the past—but he was no longer my confidante or my champion. Behind closed doors, I would write for him—my only audience who showed up on cue when inspiration struck, ready to tell me what I was doing was good, and I lapped it up like the crooning of a first love—flattery enticing me to trust him. I didn't need anyone else—an exclusive *ménage à trois* had developed between my keyboard, the devil and me.

"You think I'm talented enough to work for you then, Devil?"

"You know I do—I don't waste my time pursuing talentless prospects." He was caustically seductive.

I was a talented prospect, in the Devil's view! His intentions were clear now, he had been here to recruit me all along. Swooping in at the precious beginnings of a lone soul's creative journey—still malleable, still easily persuaded—to pluck it, fresh, out of solitude.

"Tell me Devil, how many artists work for you?"

"Thousands, my dear, most of Hollywood in fact. I look after my staff very well."

I raised my eyes to him and locked his gaze.

How would I ever know? How would I ever really know if what this sylvan-tongued tempter was telling me was true? The previously unasked question that now rose to the surface was—did I really need him? Was I brave enough to let my literary lover go for the sake of the higher moral ground, to leave the warm bed and walk out into the elements, without him?

"Make your choice, my dear, the waiting is over. What is it to be, infamy or mediocrity? Hmm?"

The artist's eternal dilemma was upon my door—in fact, he was sitting in my very own armchair, across from me. Devil versus writer. Writer versus Devil.

Again, he demanded, "Infamy or mediocrity?", his voice booming over me; the Devil—an existentialist CEO—now closing his deal.

"I choose neither, Devil," I snarled.

"Oh, no—Ha!" he laughed in condescension. "You can't not choose, my dear. You *must* choose. This is the game of life we're playing here, you *must* choose."

"Your options are so . . . " I paused, hesitating on offering him a critical viewpoint, " . . . limited," I ventured. He was silent. "I guess I want something other than what you're offering me," I said, my words wavering.

"And what would that be, my dear?"

"I want my voice heard on my own merit. Yes, that's it, Devil, that's want I want," I said clearly, the tone of the embarrassed child now gone.

The Devil stood and walked towards me, outstretching his pocked hand to cup my face. "How charmingly naive of you, my dear," he said. He squeezed my jaw slightly before brushing his hand away. "And painfully virtuous."

He reached into his coat pocket and pulled out a card, turning and dropping it on the table in front of me, before walking out with his parting words, "Call me."

I watched him walk away—the exit of the dangerous third member of my love affair. Now, I was alone with my keyboard and my bits and pieces of paper, which unflinchingly failed to flatter me for the words I produced. Just me now, alone.

Out of the corner of my eye, I saw the Devil's card on the table. I picked it up, ran my fingers over the raised gold lettering, turned it over, and started scribbling some words on the back of it.

SKIMMING STONES

Michelle Riedlinger

We sat on the park bench overlooking the river, the Devil and I. We'd been doing a lot of that lately. Sometimes I'd arrive and he'd already be there. But mostly he arrived a few minutes after me, out of breath and eager to sit.

I never asked him where he'd been. I wasn't even curious. There were things I didn't want to think about, things I didn't want to know of. These get-togethers were bad enough. We can justify almost any encounter to ourselves.

It wasn't as though he was offensive in any way. He was quite good-looking really. Not in a flashy movie star way. He was rugged, like he worked outdoors a fair bit. He always dressed well and he didn't smell bad. This is an important factor to consider when you share a park bench with someone.

Today he was waiting for me, gathering small stones from the ground and skimming them across the water. He asked me if I wanted to join him, to have a competition, but my Catholic upbringing had left me with one useful piece of guidance: never compete with the Devil.

We sat for a while in companionable silence. I liked that about him.

He didn't feel the need to make conversation for the hell of it. That was one of my failings.

"So how goes it today?" he asked: a question that a casual observer might look upon as small talk, but I knew better.

"Oh, same, same," I replied. I wasn't ready for this exchange. It had been two months since I'd been coming to the park, but I still wasn't ready. I'd recently submitted my doctoral thesis. It was a project that had taken all my time and energy and then some for four and a half years. The job was finished but, instead of feeling relieved, I felt empty and confused.

I had known this might happen after talking to other similarly dissatisfied people, but I wasn't prepared for the intensity of it. It was like looking down a deep black hole, like looking in a well and trying to see the tiniest pin. You know it is there but the more you look for it, the darker the well seems. I'd had an idea of where I was going but now I had none.

I needed a new project, something all-consuming that would overwhelm my senses. I didn't want to face this blackness. I was thirty-five and could hear my biological clock ticking for the first time. This was unsettling.

"Poor you," he said. "A child or a novel: which will it be?"

We'd had this conversation before, but he never tired of going over the intricacies of it. It was nice to have someone to listen. This was stuff I found difficult to discuss with anyone. It seemed so self-obsessed, so banal. But he didn't make me feel that way. I was begrudgingly warming to him.

"Becoming a writer seems much less painful," I said. "It seems less of a commitment, more personally fulfilling, and not so financially crippling"

"You might be right," he said. "But being a writer doesn't leave much time for anything or anyone else."

"Arrrggghhh!" I exclaimed, exasperated. "I don't see too many mothers with time on their hands. When would I find time to write? Everyone I know who has taken the road of motherhood is flat out finding time to sleep, let alone write."

I knew his answer already.

"You can have these two creative experiences at once. I can guarantee that you will be overwhelmed with them. You will lose yourself in them for a long time and they will fulfil you."

I wanted that intensity so badly.

"But you will see this blackness again," he said.

I thought about this. I was not sure I could handle the blackness of the distant future. I wasn't handling it very well now.

"Do I have to tell you now?" I asked, fully knowing the answer.

"No," he said. "There are plenty of people out there, hovering on the edges of decisions, still waiting for the answer to come to them. Some of them are on their deathbeds, thinking that they still have time to pursue some dream or other, with or without my help."

He laughed his ironic laugh. I'd come to know this laugh and preferred it when it wasn't directed at me.

"For these people the options disappeared many years before. I don't bother telling them that. They suffer just as much through not taking any action. Who am I to interfere?" he asked, more to himself than to me.

"It doesn't seem like there is much choice then," I said.

He laughed again at this, as he had done many times before.

"It is all choice," he said. "You can have things without me, but they mightn't be so easy. You'll have to juggle them all yourself and the intensity may not be there. Are you willing to take that risk? I can't tell you what Fate will do if you leave the decision to her."

"Ah," I said in response to this piece of information, probably for the twentieth time. "I think I get it."

He was sceptical. "We're going to have to do some more work together," he said, standing abruptly. "But there is hope for you."

He handed me a few small round stones. "I've got to go now, but why don't you have a practice at stone skimming while I'm gone," he suggested. "We can make a game of it next time."

I rolled my eyes, but he had already turned to go. I looked at the smooth round stones in the palm of my hand and watched him disappear down the path.

"What the hell," I thought, "no harm in practicing."

HEART AND SOUL

Nigel Stones

Joel had already bitten down all of his fingernails, so the girl with the tray of drinks had come just in time. Watching her disappear around the corner at the end of the isle, he glanced down at the paper cup he'd already drained of wine. The empty cup he held up near his chest and the wallet holding his manuscript he clasped in his other hand. Behind the shield of his forearm, he edged on. Humidity built between his left palm and the plastic of the wallet, despite the air-conditioning.

He pondered the convention centre—it was a marvel. Any interest, hobby or industry that flourished in the population of Brisbane could be housed here. No matter what and no matter what shape, they could all be contained for a few days in the box he currently wandered.

Where was he?

That's right—he was in Epic Fantasy. It didn't really matter; the aisles were all the same.

These people knew. They all had the knowledge. They were writers, publishers, agents and critics. They were all on the other side. They were there. And when they looked at him, he sensed they knew what he was.

Joel noticed a plump girl who wore a dress made of dark scraps of fabric. She sat like a hen on a plastic chair in her cubicle, accompanied by two grey cardboard display stands. The stands held copy upon copy of the same paperback, the covers projecting an absence of something and this absence was amplified by repetition. It was an indefinable not-quite-finishedness that he recognised from his high school woodworking projects and much of his own writing. Behind her, there were open boxes filled with more of the same books.

On his approach, she sat slightly more upright, colour seeming to flow into her face. He opened his mouth to speak to her but he realized, too late, that he had no idea what to say. Joel gaped for a moment like a gravid fish, then feigning recognition of someone at the other end of the aisle, he set off with contrived purpose.

It seemed, at these places, that the more you paid for your burger, the more bland and textureless it would be. Still, the coffee wasn't bad.

A shadow fell across the empty sugar packets and Joel looked up from his short black to see that he had company.

He had been joined by slightly built man with pale skin and eyes of such a dark brown that Joel had trouble discerning their pupils, even through the magnification of the finely framed spectacles they sat behind.

"Mind if I sit down, Joel?"

Joel rushed a mouthful of coffee. "Do I know you?"

"No."

"But you know me?" Joel said.

"Yes."

"But I haven't . . . "

"Published anything yet," the man cut in, "I know."

"So you're an agent then?" said Joel, now holding his cup with both hands.

The man smiled warmly. "No, I am not an agent. I would like to help you get published though."

"Who are you then?"

The man leant across the table and looked directly into Joel's eyes. "I am the Devil."

Joel pushed his chair back and stood up.

"Sit down, Joel."

This was not just a lunatic, but a pushy lunatic. "What?"

"SIT DOWN!" The voice came, not from the little man before him, but booming from every surface around. Joel felt the vibration of it through his feet and he sat down, through no voluntary action of this own.

The man covered Joel's left hand with his right. "I am sorry. I did not want to frighten you. I see this is hard for you to believe. Would you like proof?"

With a struggle, Joel nodded.

"Over my left shoulder, you will see a philodendron in a yellow planter," said the Devil, without turning around.

Again, Joel nodded.

"Watch." The Devil's smile grew as behind him the plant wilted, then its leaves began to brown and flatten. By the time the man's flawless alabaster teeth were visible, the plant was no more than a black tangle.

Joel tried to form a question, but no word came.

The Devil frowned, "Are you not convinced? Perhaps another demonstration?" He waited only briefly for a response. "The self-publisher: the girl that you avoided earlier."

"No!" said the young writer. "I believe you."

The Devil cocked his head. "I can read your thoughts, Joel."

"Really?" Joel said. "Then you should know that I'm having a bloody hard time processing this. Anyway, shouldn't you have red skin, horns and a forked tail or something?"

"I can take any form I please."

"And this form pleases you?"

Joel watched his uninvited guest, who paused to frame his answer.

"I have an engagement a little later tonight. I always like to settle into a new appearance for a while before such encounters. There are some activities during which it can be quite difficult to maintain shape."

"That's disgusting," said Joel, feeling a wave of slight dread that he could not explain move through him.

"Why, Joel? " said the Devil. "Do you think I have not needs? I am always honest with them, as I have been with you. They always want something that I am able to give them. I need to take a physical form, so why should I not take a form that they find pleasing?"

Was this really the Devil? Joel took a moment to study the man. He wore a plain white cotton shirt that should have been unremarkable, but had a crispness and sharpness of pressing that held the eye. His hair, by contrast was an untamed, unruly, raven mass. Something about its untidiness reminded Joel of a flatmate he'd once had.

"You are wasting your time with that." The Devil was looking at the green plastic wallet that held his manuscript.

"What do you mean, that it's no good?"

"No, it is actually quite good, but they will not be interested. Did you not feel it when you walked in here?"

Joel forced a frown. "What?"

"I think you know what I mean. The feeling of being different."

Joel shifted his gaze to avoid the scrutiny of his unwelcome guest.

The Devil continued. "You are different, Joel—you have a soul." He waited for the meaning in his words to penetrate, then said, "Everyone you see here has a contract with me. I own the soul of every last one of them. I am afraid they will not consider your work, fine as it is."

Perhaps it was the warm, almost avuncular manner of the man, the Devil, sitting at his table, but Joel realised that he no longer felt the course of adrenaline through his body.

"You are wondering why I would want their souls. I do like you, Joel, so I will tell you. In truth, all I really want is for them to play their part."

"Play their part in what?"

The Devil pulled a neatly folded handkerchief from his pocket, removed his glasses and began cleaning them. "Their part is to ensure the publication of speculative fiction."

"That makes no sense!"

"Joel, one day it will be my time to rule. He wants to prevent it. My adversary has done well. He has created religion and science—divide and conquer—and, whilst the masses flock to one or the other, he denies me the strength that I need. It has always been about faith, Joel. It always will be."

"I don't get it."

"Horror, fantasy, science fiction—they shape the mind. They open it like a flower to a particular kind of pollination." The Devil smiled and replaced his glasses. "Faith, Joel."

"And I guess you think you're gonna get my soul?" asked Joel.

"That is not why I sat down here," said the Devil, looking slightly wounded. "You seemed lost and, as I said, I like you."

"Bullshit!" said Joel, looking the other directly in the eyes. "You think I can't get published, but I don't need your help. And it was a monstera, not a bloody philodendron. I don't need any of this. I don't need them." He gestured at the battery farm of cubicles and the denizens of the writing industry they contained. "And, sure as hell, I don't need you."

He rose abruptly, toppling his coffee cup, sending a finger of black liquid splashing across the table and onto the white shirt of the Devil.

The Devil pulled out his handkerchief and began dabbing at the stain.

Joel stepped out of the building into the steamy January night.

"Good for you, Son. Good for you."

He heard the Devil's words carry after him, but he didn't look back.

HABERDASHERY

Kim Westwood

Down in an alleyway, in the heart of Brisbane, is a haberdashery run by a real goat of a man. I discovered it after I'd lost a girlfriend to another girlfriend, and was still feeling pretty bitter about it. But that particular day, I wasn't writing vengeance poetry; I was after a 30cm red zipper.

From the outside it didn't look good: 'Haberdashery' written in tacky serif on blacked out glass, with overly ornate gold filigree painted around the edge like an old-fashioned picture frame. *Oh lovely*, I smirked. *An olde worlde "haberdashery."* Then I noticed the doorbell really was one, and that it tinkled very pleasantly as I entered.

The proprietor was behind the counter, sorting rows of lolly jars on shelves along the back wall.

"Just browsing," I said, before he could ask. I like to be left to my own devices until I can't find what I'm looking for.

The shop went back a long way: aisles of floor-to-ceiling shelves tightly packed with little cardboard boxes, and samples of the items inside displayed on the front of the box. *Weird looking buttons*, I thought, and inspected closer. Instead of buttons, clasps or brooches there were mysteriously shaped seedpods and plant sprigs, and what could have been bits of different coloured string—but no zippers.

It's at this moment I would usually seek assistance, but as I peeked around the end of the aisle and saw the proprietor already looking my way with interest, I decided not to give him the satisfaction. So I kept wandering along the colour-coded aisles looking at the boxes and thickly wrapped embroidery reels, none of them holding the sorts of things a haberdasher would sell.

I should have walked out then and there, but a bloody-mindedness took hold. I thought of Lenore putting my unpublished poems in her shredder, and me razoring up her *Firebird* tutu, and then her doing all those private things with another girl, not me, and here I was not even able to get a zipper. So I grabbed a box from the shelf with a bunch of claw-shaped sprigs on its front, and another box further along with stringy red bits, and marched with them to the counter.

"I'll have some of both of these thanks," I said brusquely to the guy, not wanting to look him in the face. He was extremely goaty, but had expertly applied some makeup to soften the impact.

"Ahhh," he said in a resonant and mellifluent tone, holding up the clawed twigs. "Henbane, eh? Naaasty."

And then he laughed like a girl.

This, of course, pleased me, and I warmed to him slightly.

He began to separate several strands of the red string from the boxful, and then looked at me, arching one well-plucked eyebrow. "Heartsache: love gone wrong, carbuncles, flatulence—"

"Well I only want it for the *first* one of those," I said, insulted that he might think of me as flatulent.

"Tell you what," he fixed me with a concerned blue eye. "I can see you're in genuine need. I'll give you the lot for free—gift wrapping included—if you'll let me take your soul and pop it in a jar." He had clearly sussed my thrifty nature.

I looked at the name-tagged jars behind him. They were all empty. "Fine by me," I replied in a devil-may-care mood.

He took a lustreware jar and a blank label from beneath the counter, and winked.

"So . . . is that Alice with an 'i' or a 'y'?"

The goaty man stuck the label on the jar, and set it in a space on a high shelf. Then he put my purchases in an enviro-friendly brown paper bag tied with string in two neat bows.

"Careful where you apply those," he called after me. "And if you need any help, you know where I am."

Somehow I knew he really meant it—and that he didn't mean the RACQ type of help (which is the sort of help that, say you have four flat tyres and they have been slashed instead of gone down accidentally, *won't* help in this instance). Still, I didn't intend ever going back—until the heartsache remedy backfired and I gave myself a hefty dose of carbuncles.

"You've still got a lot of anger in you," Mr Goat said as I stalked towards his counter in my freshly constructed red tulle culottes and matching satin bolero. "And holding it all in like that is very unhealthy—it's a wonder you haven't developed lockjaw as well."

"Yeah, well, I've got a lot to be angry about."

"Like what?" he asked interestedly.

"Like you're not a real haberdashery."

"Well, that would depend on what you understand by 'real', and by 'haberdashery'."

"Why don't you have zippers then?"

"Don't need to." He waved mildly at the jars, all different shapes and sizes, ascending the wall of shelves behind him. "And I must say, Brisbane has been very good for business."

I looked at my pearly one tucked in amongst the others.

"But they're all empty," I snorted. Clearly he was delusional.

He smiled. "That depends on what you understand by—"

"Shut up!" I shouted and slammed the glass door, its bell tinkly and musical, behind me.

Next time I went back it was at midnight, with a slingshot.

I snuck in so craftily that the bell tinkled just once, softly. My slingshot was from a specialist weaponry supplier: industrial, accurate. I aimed, and *WAP!* the pearly jar shattered.

I waited. Nothing.

"You can't get it back, I'm afraid." Goat Face wandered into the shop from a back room. "It'd be like stuffing a minotaur into a mousehole."

"But it's mine!"

"You've moved on—I'd sit back and enjoy the sea change," he said as he got out another jar and attached the old label to it.

All I felt was grumpy.

"Would one of these make you feel better?" He dumped a large cardboard box onto the counter, and out tumbled a bunch of fluffy wombats, long-snouted bilbys and wall-eyed koalas.

"No, it wouldn't," I said snappily, and left. But I didn't slam the door; I closed it carefully, so as not to get my culottes caught in the jamb. Then I shouted "Damned if I'm coming back here again!" from halfway down the alley.

But I wasn't away long.

I missed the quiet dingy aisles of boxes, the dust and strange smells—and, to be honest, the company. I also missed being close to my soul, sitting invisibly in its replacement lolly jar.

"Well, hellooo stranger," Mr Goat purrs, silky nice, as I walk in.

"Yes, yes, I'm back," I reply, bright and dark at the same time.

He leans conversationally across the counter. "How's the writing?"

"Spiffing. I've lost my anonymity—*Poetry of the Damned* is selling like hotcakes and now they want me to unveil installation art."

"Excellent!"

"But the words have lost all their meaning." I glance at the jar. "Can't I just have a bit back, or something?"

"No such thing as half a soul." He puts on a stripy maitre d' apron. "How about a coffee? I've just closed a deal on a brand new state-of-the-art cappuccino machine."

It takes up the rest of the counter, all chrome and black, 'Diablo' written in flowing script across its front.

Great, now he thinks he's a barista. I feel decidedly ungenerous, but I say yes.

"Just a quick one, then."

He smiles broadly—the word "quick" always seems to amuse him.

"I thought I'd got over my soul being in a jar," I say, "when you gave Lenore carbuncles instead of me."

"Ahh, well, I can't take any credit for what I didn't do—that was all your cleverness."

Even minus a soul, I feel mildly uncomfortable at the thought of being responsible for Lenore dancing the lead role in *Sleeping Beauty* with pustular sores, and change the topic.

"How come I never see anyone else in here?"

"I like to take the personal approach—going one-on-one in business is always so much more fulfilling, don't you think?"

He carries a tray of coffee and chocolate-coated digestives out the door. I follow, stepping below the bell.

"Kitsch," I mutter, but genuinely attracted to the sound.

We sit smoking in the alleyway at a little mosaicked café table—another of his recent innovations.

"Just like you get at the arty bookshops," he says, smoke wafting gently from his nose, eyes and ears.

He lifts a fine-boned hirsute leg and, resting it on the table, starts to shine the hoof with a polishing cloth.

"Show-off," I say.

"You could do this too—if you spent some time stretching your hamstrings and adductors."

"Not likely." I'm focussed on the hoof.

The aroma of coffee rises; the alleyway cobblestones glint. Just for a moment memory floats above me, a light-splecked phantom in the after-sun gloom, and I recall that Brisbane was only ever meant to be a brief stop to buy a zipper, and that once, I had another life—down south somewhere, I think.

THE DIABOLIC BLOCK

Mirjana Zivkovic

Sitting at a school desk once again. Well, not exactly a real one, but I still feel like a schoolboy. I was the first to arrive, of course, so I sat in the last row to keep an eye on the competition. No one's going to peek over my shoulder and steal my ideas.

This masterclass has really got me excited. It never occurred to me before to sign up for something like this. I'm ashamed to admit how much time I spent last night picking out the clothes to wear today. I hesitated for a long time between a black turtleneck sweater and a white shirt with a bow tie. In the end I didn't wear either one and chose something that turned out to be right on mark, take my word for it. I clipped my nails too—they could have torn all this paper in front of me to shreds—and put some drops in my eyes after noticing they weren't burning with enough conviction.

I looked at the others knowingly as they entered and took great pleasure in trying to guess which one would be the first to cry out to me. Poor things, they'd really set their hearts on this masterclass. Each one wondered what would happen: if his story were pronounced the best . . . if someone were to buy hers . . . if hers, out of all the others, were to be turned into a movie. You know, I felt sorry for them because they didn't stand a chance with me there. All I can say is that I was quite pleased with myself. Each of them just gave a compassionate, fleeting look at the guy in Bermudas and a t-shirt sitting in the last row, then forgot him the same instant. They clearly felt he didn't pose the slightest threat to them and continued eyeing each other surreptitiously. That was exactly the effect I'd wanted to achieve. That's why I didn't wear either the black turtleneck or the white shirt with a bow tie. I even left my notorious stick with its death's head handle at home.

Up to that point everything had been in perfect order if you asked me. And then the writer came in who was holding the masterclass and slipped me my first surprise. After introducing himself, talking a bit with the participants, and reading his story entitled "Telephone", he said, "You have one hour to write a story about a writer and the devil in Brisbane."

What a sneaky devil, I thought, forgetting for a moment who was the real devil. I had to give him credit for his choice of topic; the man had a truly subtle feeling for what's important. I also had to admit that I was thrilled and flattered that he'd asked the participants to write about me, that is he was asking me to write about myself. I've always harboured the greatest love for myself. I thought, it's like this man has read my thoughts (something that's actually in my line of work, as you know, but let's put that aside for the moment, I'll look into it later). That was the reason I'd signed up for this masterclass. I'd secretly hoped I'd have a chance to tell the world, even in a roundabout way, something about myself that was other than common knowledge.

"Ladies and gentlemen, you may begin."

My eyes swept over the other participants once again and I smiled derisively. They were all just wannabe writers and I was the devil. When would they realize they had no business being there?

I picked up my pen . . .

. . . "Ladies and gentlemen, the time is up. Please turn in your work!"

Come again, what's that, wait a minute! Why, I haven't even started!

What happened? A whole hour couldn't possibly have passed already. And then I understood. Once again I hadn't been able to resist. Curiosity would truly bring my demise one day. I'd simply had to see what they were writing about me. So I got to talking to each one of the participants, regardless of whether or not they'd summoned me, in the hopes of getting a chance to foist my legendary contract on them whereby they'd turn over their souls to me one day.

I'd had to debate with one man whether or not he really wanted to see his work published. I'd had to convince one of the ladies that not even I was able to remove all past competition so she could be quite certain that everything she wrote was original. Just imagine, one of them even thought to ask me to do away with all the distractions that prevent honourable writers from devoting themselves solely to writing. Have you ever heard of willpower, dear writers?

I'd been nonetheless forced to sidestep one of the participants because I'd presented myself to him falsely some twenty years ago. I was certain that he wouldn't believe a thing I whispered to him unless I gave it to him in writing. I'd even had to kill in order to prove to one of them that I exist.

Then I realized that I'd wasted a great deal of time racking my brains over how to get a woman to consent to eternal suffering in the life hereafter in exchange for the canines she offered, and to prove to someone enamoured of his own ideas that it would be much more profitable if he were to accept mine. But for me the greatest challenge was the lady who felt that writing was an elemental part of her life. I used every means available to convince her to write something in my name that would shock the world.

The only surprise, other than that provided by the writer holding the masterclass, came from the lady who entered unobserved and sat right next to the door. I hadn't expected her there. I thought that this was probably my last chance to convince her to forget about Fate and entrust the management of her life to me . . .

I might have been able to push back the hands on the clock some fifteen minutes. That would have been enough time to think up some-thing ... yes, I could have done that, but the crux of the problem was that not a single idea had crossed my mind the whole time. That's why I'd peered over everyone else's shoulder and struck up a conversation with each one of them. Where was that devil when I needed him? I left with my tail between my legs after turning in a blank piece of paper.

I'm sure that during the lunch break I'll think of something that will blow them all away. It will be a simple job to slip the lecturer a new piece of paper when we return to the classroom.

Translated from the Serbian by Alice Copple-Tosic

Printed in the United States
54245LVS00002B/118